"Whoever did th[...] dangerous," Gra[...]

Eve leaned into him. "If you're saying that just to frighten me, it's working."

He forced himself to release his hold on her. It was either that or pull her close and kiss that terrified look away. "If you see anyone suspicious, you call me."

"Do you think I'm in danger?"

He wanted to reassure her that she would be fine, that he would never let anyone harm her. But he respected her too much to lie to her. "You're probably fine. But I like to exercise what we call an abundance of caution."

"Does this mean I'm going to see you again?"

The question caught him off guard. "Would you like that?"

A ghost of a smile played about her full lips. "If I am in danger, you look like a handy man to have around."

He knew a challenge when he heard one. "I plan on sticking close."

He'd leave it up to Eve how close he could get.

MOUNTAIN OF EVIDENCE

CINDI MYERS

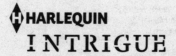

For Gay and Reed

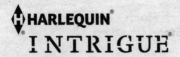

INTRIGUE

Recycling programs
for this product may
not exist in your area.

ISBN-13: 978-1-335-13690-9

Mountain of Evidence

Copyright © 2020 by Cynthia Myers

This edition published by arrangement with Harlequin Books S.A.

For questions and comments about the quality of this book,
please contact us at CustomerService@Harlequin.com.

Harlequin Enterprises ULC
22 Adelaide St. West, 40th Floor
Toronto, Ontario M5H 4E3, Canada
www.Harlequin.com

Printed in U.S.A.

Cindi Myers is the author of more than fifty novels. When she's not crafting new romance plots, she enjoys skiing, gardening, cooking, crafting and daydreaming. A lover of small-town life, she lives with her husband and two spoiled dogs in the Colorado mountains.

Books by Cindi Myers

Harlequin Intrigue

The Ranger Brigade: Rocky Mountain Manhunt

Investigation in Black Canyon
Mountain of Evidence

Eagle Mountain Murder Mystery: Winter Storm Wedding

Ice Cold Killer
Snowbound Suspicion
Cold Conspiracy
Snowblind Justice

Eagle Mountain Murder Mystery

Saved by the Sheriff
Avalanche of Trouble
Deputy Defender
Danger on Dakota Ridge

The Ranger Brigade: Family Secrets

Murder in Black Canyon
Undercover Husband
Manhunt on Mystic Mesa
Soldier's Promise
Missing in Blue Mesa
Stranded with the Suspect

Visit the Author Profile page at Harlequin.com.

CAST OF CHARACTERS

Commander Grant Sanderlin—The divorced father of two has recently taken charge of the Ranger Brigade. He's fed up with Dane Trask's games of hide-and-seek and hopes Eve can provide some answers.

Eve Shea—Dane's former lover wants marriage and a family—something Dane wasn't willing to give. She broke up with him and is trying to start fresh, but a mysterious letter from Dane pulls her into the mystery of his disappearance.

Dane Trask—This former army ranger has disappeared in the wilds of Black Canyon of the Gunnison National Park. Why did he leave his job as a successful engineer for TDC Enterprises and abandon those who care about him?

Toby Masterson—Dane's former colleague at TDC is pursuing Eve. He and Dane have a lot in common. Will Eve be one more thing they share?

Mitch Ruffino—The TDC vice president alternately praises and condemns Dane Trask and has offered a large reward for his capture.

Chapter One

Missing Man: Presumed Dangerous
$25,000 Reward!

The bold announcement on the poster tacked to the
post office bulletin board was enough to catch the
attention of almost every patron who waited in line,
but it was the photo beneath the words that made
Eve Shea's stomach sink. The dark-haired man with
the chiseled features of an outdoorsman and determined blue eyes looked out from what was probably
a company ID photo, but in the context of the poster
looked more like a mug shot.

Wanted: Dane Trask
43, 6'2", 180 lb.
Blue eyes, dark brown hair
Armed and dangerous
**If you know anything about the whereabouts of
this man, call the number below.**

Dane, where are you, and what have you done? Eve thought as she stared at the picture of her former lover—the man she had once dreamed of marrying. Though she and Dane had agreed to stop seeing each other six months ago, Eve couldn't help but feel for him. He hadn't been the man she needed, but she had believed he was a good man, and now the news reports were saying that he had done terrible things—embezzled money from his employer, and even committed acts of terrorism. Could she really have loved a terrorist?

"Ma'am? It's your turn." The man behind her in line got Eve's attention and nodded toward the front counter, where a clerk waited, deep frown lines furrowing her brow.

"Oh! Sorry." Eve hurried to the counter and handed over her parcel to be weighed.

Dane was still on her mind as she exited the building a few moments later and started the short walk to the flower shop she owned on Main Street in Montrose, Colorado. The last time she had heard from him had been two months ago, when he had texted to wish her a happy birthday. It was just like him to remember and acknowledge the date. "I understand we can't be lovers," he had said when they ended their three-year relationship. "But I'll always be your friend."

A knot formed in her throat at the memory. In some ways, the split might have been easier if he had been a jerk about it, but that just wasn't Dane. He wasn't the type to act out of anger or spite. Looking back, she could say that was one of the reasons things hadn't worked out between them—Dane was always so controlled. She had wanted passion, romance, an undying commitment.

She had wanted a baby. And Dane had been adamant that he had no desire to be a father again. He adored his daughter, Audra, but she was twenty-three and he had no interest in raising another child. It was the one big difference they simply couldn't get past.

She pushed open the door to Eve's Garden and an electronic chime announced her entry. She breathed in the scents of fresh roses and carnations and some of the tension in her shoulders eased. A trio of fountains burbled in the corner and a pyramid of ivy, ferns and other green plants basked in the light streaming through the front display window. Fresh flower arrangements awaited buyers from a bank of lighted coolers, and racks of greeting cards and shelves of small gift items invited browsing. Everything about this place was peaceful and beautiful, the product of her inspiration and hard work.

"Good morning." Sarah Maclean, a tall forty-something woman who wore her blond hair in a pixie cut, emerged from the shop's back room. Eve had hired Sarah as her first full-time employee two years ago. She hadn't been looking to take on any help but Sarah, who had experience as a floral designer and a desire to go back to work once her youngest child entered high school, had persuaded Eve that she would be an asset to the business. Which, indeed, she was. "I've got the arrangements for the Women's Club luncheon ready to go, and I just sent Manuel out with the orders for First Bank and Hightower Financial," Sarah said.

"Thanks," Eve said, passing through to behind the front counter. "I'd say you're far too energetic this early in the morning, but I'd be a fool to complain."

"I never can sleep past six and I like to keep busy," Sarah said. "Oh, and I stopped by the post office on my way in and collected the mail from our box. It's on your desk."

Eve had been so shaken by Dane's wanted poster she had forgotten to even check the post office box. "I'll go through the mail, then start working on the order for the Salazar wedding and reception," she said. The wedding and subsequent banquet would require an extra shipment of roses, lilies, stephanotis, and trailing ivy for the bride's bouquet, six brides-maids' bouquets, boutonnieres for the groom, father of the bride, attendants and ushers, corsages for the mothers of the bride and groom, a hair wreath for the flower girl, four large arrangements for the front of the church, and ten table arrangements for the reception, plus small swags for the buffet tables. It could easily be Eve's largest commission of the year.

"All right, but first I want to know how your date

went on Friday night." Sarah picked up her coffee cup and leaned back against the counter, as if in anticipation of a long chat. "Was he as good-looking as his picture online? Did the two of you hit it off?"

Eve had to think a moment to recall what Sarah was talking about. Friday already seemed so long ago. She shrugged. "He was okay, but I doubt I'll see him again."

Sarah's shoulders and face sagged with disappointment. "What happened? Why wouldn't he want to see you again? You're so nice, and funny, and is he blind, because honestly, you're gorgeous."

Eve laughed. "You might be a little bit biased." In addition to running the shop with the organization only a mother of four could bring, Sarah was intent on whipping Eve's life into shape. She wasn't overly pushy, just Eve's number one champion and cheerleader. "Nothing happened. Not really." That was part of the problem. Doug Howard had been a well-mannered, good-looking, friendly guy who owned a local pest control company. He was divorced with two boys, and seemed like a good father and a very nice man. But Eve had felt zero attraction to him and by the end of the evening was counting the minutes until she could politely say good-night.

"No sparks, huh?" Sarah looked sympathetic. "Don't you worry, hon. You keep putting yourself out there and you'll find the right man."

Eve nodded. "I won't stop trying, I promise."

After her split with Dane, she and Sarah had devised what they called "the plan." Eve had registered for two online dating sites, and discreetly put the word out to friends that she was interested in meeting eligible men who were ready to settle down and start a family. She reasoned that the more candidates for "the one" she auditioned, the more likely she was to meet her Mr. Right. It was a little like interviewing a candidate for a job—the most important job she could imagine—her life partner and the father of her children.

But in six months of going out at least once and often twice a week, she hadn't even come up with one possible finalist for the position.

"What about Saturday?" Sarah asked. "Did you go out Saturday night?"

"Saturday I stayed home." She had binge-watched romantic movies, eaten ice cream and, frankly, felt sorry for herself.

"All this stuff with Dane has you upset, doesn't it?" Sarah asked. She knew the whole story of Dane and Eve's ill-fated relationship. Eve sometimes thought her friend mourned the break-up harder than Eve had. Now Sarah's expressive features twisted into a look of horror and pity. "The news stories are just horrible, but you have to ignore them. Dane isn't part of your life anymore. You have to move on."

"Dane will always be part of my life," she said. "A part that's in the past, but I can't just ignore the fact that he's missing and no one knows whether he's dead or alive. And that he's been accused of horrible things. That isn't like the man I know at all."

"I saw a notice at the post office this morning," Sarah said. "Offering a $25,000 reward for information about Dane's whereabouts. The poster said he's dangerous. Do you think that's true?"

Was Dane dangerous? He certainly hadn't been to her. But he had been an army ranger, and he was athletic and fit, and knew how to handle a gun. For some unknown reason, he had left his job almost a month ago, saying he was headed for a hike in Black Canyon of the Gunnison National Park. And he hadn't been heard from since. Park rangers found his black Ford pickup at the bottom of the canyon, but they hadn't found his body or his backpack, which led some people to believe Dane had tried to fake his own death.

But why?

"You're not answering me," Sarah said. "Does that mean you think Dane *is* dangerous?"

"No!" Eve protested. "I just…" She shrugged. "Before all this, I would have said I knew Dane pretty well. Now, I don't know what to think."

"I always liked him," Sarah said. "Even if I did think he took you for granted. And I never understood why he was so reluctant to have more children. I mean, he and Audra get along great. You'd think he would want to repeat the experience."

It was an old argument, one Eve no longer wanted to hear. "I can't worry about Dane now. I have to get to work."

She moved to the tiny kitchen off the workspace and poured a cup of coffee from the pot Sarah had started earlier, then carried it to her desk in the equally tiny office. There was just enough room in there for a desk, a filing cabinet and a desk chair. Any visitors to the office had to stand in the doorway to speak to her.

She switched on her computer, then began sorting the pile of mail on the desk blotter. A floral supply catalog, two flyers from printing companies, an announcement about a florists' convention, a reminder about a seasonal sale from one of her suppliers, a bill from a wholesaler and a small pile of ads and come-ons she transferred straight to the recycling bin under the desk.

At the bottom of the pile was a nine-by-twelve manila envelope. When she turned it over to read the address on the front, she stopped breathing for a moment. The envelope didn't have a return address, but the handwriting for her name and PO box was familiar to her from birthday and Valentine's cards over the past few years.

Hand trembling, she picked up the silver letter opener embossed with the name of a floral wholesaler—a trade show freebie from last year—and slit open the envelope. She slid out a single sheet of paper.

FOR IMMEDIATE RELEASE
TDC Enterprises Falsifies Reports in
Major Environmental Fraud

The press release that followed charged TDC with lying about contaminant levels at a mine site they had contracted to clean up as part of the federal government's Superfund cleanup program. TDC had been awarded a hefty chunk of taxpayer money to return the contaminated Mary Lee Mine to an environmentally safe condition, free of arsenic, mercury, sulfuric acid and other hazardous chemicals that had leached into soil and water on or near the site over the years.

Instead of using the government funds to remove contaminants from the site, this press release charged TDC with adding even more contaminants, and then lying about everything in official reports.

Eve read through the release twice, her wariness growing. Unlike the traditional press releases that had crossed her desk in the three years she had worked for the *Montrose Daily Press* prior to opening this shop, this one contained no contact information, or sources for these allegations.

She picked up the envelope again and examined it. Something hard lay inside. She upended the envelope and a brass key landed on the desk with a *thunk*. Pain squeezed her heart as she stared at the key. She had one just like it, tucked away in the jewelry box on top of her dresser at home. Dane had given her that key. Why was he sending her its mate now?

Chapter Two

"Dane Trask is becoming a huge pain in the keister." Ranger Brigade Commander Grant Sanderlin would have preferred to use stronger language to describe the current focus of his force's efforts, but he had given up swearing for Lent and, after a lecture from his ex-wife about watching his mouth around their daughters, he was trying to keep up the practice. Dane Trask's efforts to frustrate his pursuers at every turn were making that more of a challenge.

"Trask is annoying," Lieutenant Randall Knightbridge agreed from his position at the conference table to Grant's right. Knightbridge's full-sleeve tattoos peeking beneath the cuffs of his uniform shirt reminded Grant of the skateboarders his oldest daughter used to date. But in Grant's first month in command of the Ranger Brigade, he had learned that Knightbridge's deep-set dark eyes didn't miss a thing. "But Terrell, Davis and Compton are just as bad."

Yes, TDC Enterprises, Trask's employer and the

chief source of the allegations against him, had managed to insert themselves into the investigation in ways that grated. Their insistence on offering a $25,000 reward for Trask's apprehension, and then bypassing law enforcement altogether and setting up their own information hotline, meant the Rangers weren't privy to any information TDC received about Trask unless the company decided to share it. And more recently, two killers who may or may not have been TDC employees had tried to murder one of Grant's officers and the woman who was now, apparently, that officer's fiancée.

"We're still trying to find out more about the men who attacked Officer Beck and Cara Mead," Officer Carmen Redhorse, on Grant's left, said. Grant thought of the sharp and fearless Redhorse, a native Ute, as the most tenacious of the officers under his new command. She wouldn't stop searching until she had discovered all there was to know about the two killers. "TDC isn't being very cooperative, and a judge refused to grant us a warrant for their employment records," Redhorse continued.

"Keep talking to everyone who had contact with Walter George and Anthony Durrell at TDC," Grant said. "Someone knows if TDC was as ignorant of the men's histories as they say, or if they hired them as killers." He looked around the table. "What else have we got?"

"The latest test results from the Mary Lee Mine

show contamination with radioactive material." Jason Beck, a new member of the team who had been assigned to the Ranger Brigade from the US Park Police, spoke up. Tall, with close-cropped brown hair, Beck looked younger than his twenty-nine years. "There are no radioactive elements occurring naturally in that area, so it's possible TDC brought them in—either knowingly or unknowingly—in all the waste rock that's been dumped there."

"TDC contends that those reports are evidence Trask stored illegal nuclear material at the mine." Lieutenant Michael Dance, muscular and intense, spoke from the other end of the conference table.

"But as yet they haven't offered any explanation of how or where he obtained this mysterious material," Beck said. "Or how they would know about it."

"It's an interesting puzzle," Grant said. "But the Montrose County Sheriff's Department and Homeland Security are involved in investigating the terrorism allegations against Trask. Our focus is on finding the missing man, since he disappeared from our jurisdiction and the few suspicious sightings we've had seem to indicate he's still here."

"Here" was over 130,000 acres of public land that included the National Park, Curecanti National Recreation Area and Gunnison Gorge National Conservation Area. A lot of very empty country, much of it without roads, where the former army ranger might be camping out.

"It could explain why Trask disappeared in the first place," Beck said. "Though Montrose hasn't been very forthcoming with any information they might have, and Homeland Security sure isn't going to share whatever they have."

"That is about to change, at least on the Montrose side of things," Grant said. He strode to the door and opened it. "Deputy Martin, you can join us now."

Montrose County Sheriff's Deputy Faith Martin, a few brown curls escaping her tight bun, surveyed her new colleagues warily. Grant imagined the petite, feminine officer had had to prove herself over and over again in what had been, as far as the reports he received indicated, an unblemished career as a law enforcement officer. "Deputy Martin is our new liaison with the sheriff's department," Grant said. "Deputy Martin, please report on the department's progress in their investigation into the charges against Dane Trask."

Martin nodded, took the empty chair beside Knightbridge, and proceeded to speak without notes, in a calm contralto voice. "TDC has shared security footage they attest shows Trask smuggling uranium ore from another site they're in the process of mitigating," she said. "One near Uravan, Colorado, an area of active uranium mining in the forties and fifties."

"Attest?" Beck asked.

Martin shrugged. "He's carrying a rock. The

video is poor quality, so we can't tell if it's really uranium ore. Someone suggested it might be waste rock Trask was testing as part of his job duties, but someone has convinced Homeland Security that is not the case."

"Even if Trask did take old uranium ore from a defunct mine, it wouldn't be high enough quality to make anything useful to a terrorist," Dance said. "It's one reason those mines played out."

"Maybe the terrorist doesn't know that," Mark "Hud" Hudson said. Another new recruit, he was the team's tech expert, though his muscular build and fondness for sports belied the usual geek image. "Maybe Trask is pulling a fast one on them."

"TDC has pulled back their allegations against Trask's admin, Cara Mead, at least for the time being," Martin said. "Apparently whatever evidence they had against her was circumstantial, at best."

Jason Beck, Cara Mead's fiancé, mumbled something under his breath. Grant sent him a warning look and he sat up straighter in his chair. "Thank you, Deputy Martin," Grant said.

Grant consulted his meeting notes. He was about to dismiss the group when a knock on the door interrupted. "Come in," he called.

One of the three civilians who served as administrative support for the team—Sylvia—peered around the door. "I'm sorry to interrupt, but there's a woman here who says she needs to speak to whoever is in charge of the Dane Trask case. She says it's urgent."

The energy level in the room immediately rose. Grant knew better than to hope they might be a little closer to getting Dane Trask out of their hair, but sometimes you did get lucky. "Put her in my office," he said. "I'll be right there."

All of his officers were working on this case, but if this woman wanted to speak to the person in charge, that would be him. Dane Trask might be a pain in the keister, but he was Grant's pain.

Chapter Three

Striking. It wasn't a word Grant had used to describe a woman before, but it fit Eve Shea perfectly. She had thick, honey-colored hair that flowed past her shoulders, and was mussed by the wind, not so much styled as somewhat tamed by the tortoise shell clips that held it back on each side of her face. And what a face—dark, thick brows above wide-set hazel eyes and a nose that was maybe larger than considered conventionally beautiful, and a sharp chin. The strong features suited her. He estimated she was in her middle thirties—young, but not too young. She wasn't a large woman, but she carried herself with the air of woman who was prepared at any moment to kick butt and take names.

"I'm Commander Grant Sanderlin," he said after Sylvia had introduced his visitor and left.

Ms. Shea shook his hand with a firm grip. He released her hand reluctantly, her skin smooth and cool against his own. He motioned for her to sit and took his own chair. "What can I do for you, Ms. Shea?"

"If you're investigating this case, you already know Dane Trask and I dated for three years. We split up six months ago."

Grant felt the sensation of something clicking into place in his mind. He'd been so distracted by this woman's presence that he had failed to register the significance of her name. One of his officers—Hudson, he thought—had interviewed her shortly after Trask was reported missing. "Do you have some new information for us?" Grant asked. "Has Trask contacted you?"

The sudden tightness around her mouth made him think his words had touched a nerve. She opened the large leather satchel slung over one shoulder and withdrew a manila envelope. "I received this in the mail this morning," she said, handing the envelope across the desk. "The handwriting on the envelope is Dane's—or a very good forgery."

Grant slipped on his reading glasses—the fact that he had to use them in the past few months still grated. He took a pair of nitrile gloves from his desk drawer and slipped them on before he slid the single sheet of paper onto the desk and studied it. "What is this?" he asked after a moment.

"It's a press release," she said. "Or, at least, it's in the style of a press release. I used to work as a reporter for the *Montrose Daily Press* and I probably had hundreds of these come across my desk in my time there. Though they usually include contact information to allow the reporter to follow up on the story. This one doesn't."

Grant skimmed the document again. "Why do you think Trask sent this to you?"

"I don't know. Maybe he wants me to take it to my former employer and ask them to publish it. But I can't do that."

He looked at her, one eyebrow raised in silent question.

"It would be totally irresponsible to print something this inflammatory," she said. "Especially without any proof."

"Maybe he's expecting you to find the proof," Grant said. "Or he thinks you already have it."

"I own a flower shop. I haven't worked as a reporter for quite a while, and I don't have a connection to TDC."

"Then I have to ask again—why did Trask send this to you?"

The tightness around her mouth became a frown. She reached into her purse again. "This was in the envelope, too."

He took the small brass key. "It looks like the key to a safe deposit box," he said.

"Yes." She let out a long breath. "I have one like it in my jewelry box at home. I'd forgotten all about it until I received this one."

"What's the significance of the key?" Grant

asked. "You said you and Trask had broken up—
yet you still had the key to a joint safe deposit box?"

"Not a joint box—this belonged to Dane. And
the only reason I still have a key is that he gave it to
me so long ago I think we both forgot all about it.
Or at least, I did."

"Go on. Why did he give you the key in the first
place?"

"It was after we had been seeing each other for
about a year, when it felt like things were serious between us. He asked me if I would mind being a signatory on his safe deposit box. That would allow me
to access the box in the event something happened
to him. He said the box contained his will and some
other legal documents and that he could count on me
to handle everything properly for him."

"Was he anticipating something happening?"
Grant asked. "Was he ill, or had he mentioned threats
from someone?"

"Nothing like that. That was just how Dane was—
how he *is*. He's prepared for any eventuality, and he's
usually thinking two steps ahead of everyone else."

"You agreed to be responsible for his affairs if
something happened to him?"

"Yes. He didn't think his daughter, Audra, was
old enough to deal with those things. She was barely
twenty at the time." She shrugged. "And I thought
he was the man I'd marry. The request to do this for
him wasn't unreasonable."

"If things were so serious between the two of you, why did you end the relationship?" Did Trask have another woman in his life they should question? Or a secret vice that might have led him to abandon his everyday life?

"He didn't feel the same way about marriage and family as I did," she said. "We parted amicably and remained friends." She nodded toward the envelope on the desk in front of Grant. "Maybe that's why he sent that to me. He needed help and turned to a friend."

Grant examined the key more closely. "Did you ever see the contents of the box?" he asked.

She shook her head. "We went to the bank and I signed some papers and got the key, but I never opened the box. I really had forgotten all about it."

"When you received this key this morning, did you go to the bank and open the box?"

"No. I came straight here."

Smart woman—if she was telling the truth, and that should be easy enough to verify. Banks recorded everything. "Which bank?"

"Community United," she said.

He made note of the name, then studied her for a long moment. She pretended not to notice his scrutiny, instead focusing on the photograph on the credenza behind him, of him with both his daughters. "Are those your children?" she asked.

"Yes." He could have left it there, but added,

"Beth is seventeen and Janie is fifteen. They live with their mother in DC." *And I don't see nearly enough of them.*

"They're very pretty girls."

He would have liked to talk with this woman about his daughters, one of his favorite topics, especially now that he lived so far from them, but he forced himself to focus on the task at hand. "What kind of a relationship did you have with Trask?" he asked.

"Pardon me?" A hint of frost tinged her voice.

"I'm trying to get into this man's head, to think like he thinks. To try to figure out his next move. At one time not that long ago you were closer to him than probably anyone else. Maybe you can help me understand him more fully."

Some of the tension eased from her body. "Dane is very intelligent, very capable. He's the kind of person who excels at everything he does. He makes everything look easy. He's very calm and dependable. He's not one to fly into rages or act impulsively." She leaned forward. "Disappearing like this—it's not like him. When Dane does something, he's thought about it a long time and come up with a plan. He doesn't act rashly."

"He sounds perfect." Grant couldn't keep the note of derision from his voice. "Who initiated the breakup between the two of you?"

"How is that pertinent?"

"You said he was the type to plan things. Maybe breaking up with you was part of his preparations to disappear."

"Our splitting up wasn't his idea, it was mine. But I don't think Dane was surprised when I told him I couldn't date him anymore."

"Was he upset about it? Did he try to talk you into reconsidering?"

"No."

And that hurt, didn't it? Grant thought. If you were with someone for three years, he ought to at least protest a little. "Dane wasn't one to argue with a decision," she said, as if to defend Trask. "He could see I'd made up my mind and he respected that."

"Did you keep in touch?"

"A couple of times after that I ran into him in town. And I got a text from him on my birthday."

"When was that?"

"January 10."

"Do you know if Trask dated anyone after the two of you split?"

"Your officer asked me that and the answer is, I don't know. I didn't keep up with his personal life."

She was giving him another "that is none of your business" stare, but he had to get past people's barriers to the information they possessed that would help him do his job. "What was your first thought when you saw the envelope?" he asked.

"I was afraid."

The answer surprised him. Eve Shea didn't strike him as a woman who frightened easily. "Why was that? Did you feel Trask was a threat to you? Has he ever threatened you before, or tried to harm you?" He could taste the anger at the thought at the back of his throat, and inhaled deeply to beat it back. He was interviewing a potential witness, not defending a crime victim.

"Dane would never hurt me!" Her shock at the idea rang clear in the words.

"Yet you were afraid when you saw the envelope, addressed to you in Trask's handwriting."

"I'd seen a poster at the post office shortly before. It said Dane was dangerous and offered a $25,000 reward for information on his whereabouts. The idea that someone believes he's dangerous, and is offering that kind of money to track him down…" Her words trailed away and she shook her head. "I was frightened for Dane—knowing he had people hunting him like that. And I thought…" She paused and wet her lips. "I thought if he was getting in touch with me, he must be really desperate."

"You still care about him," Grant said, keeping his voice very even, with no hint of emotion.

"Of course I care about him. He's a friend and he's out there somewhere, alone, unable to defend himself against all these accusations."

"You don't believe the charges against him."

"Dane Trask is the last person in the world who

would be a terrorist or have anything to do with terrorists," she said. "He was a soldier, a real patriot. He wasn't cynical or snide about it, either. Dane really does love his country. As for the embezzlement claims—it's ridiculous. Dane had money. He wasn't in debt. I never heard him wish for more money or talk about getting rich or anything like that. And he loved his work. He would never steal, and he certainly wouldn't steal from an employer."

"So you think TDC is making up the story?"

"I don't know what to think, but Dane didn't steal from them. He just wouldn't."

Grant slid the letter into the envelope once more, then stripped off the gloves. "We'll look into this. Thank you for bringing it to our attention."

"I'd like to be with you when you open the deposit box," she said.

"I thought you didn't want to know what was in it," he said. "That's why you were turning this over to us."

"I didn't want to be by myself when I found out the contents," she said. "But of course I want to know."

"I don't see the need to involve you any further," he said.

She stood, and he thought she would leave. Instead, she met his gaze, her expression all determination. "In order to open that box, you'll need a warrant," she said. "That takes time. As a signatory on the account, I can open the box for you," she said. "Won't that make things quicker?"

He could have countered her argument with one of his own—that obtaining a warrant shouldn't be difficult, since Dane was a crime suspect and a missing person. Instead, he nodded, intrigued. "All right," he said. "You can come with me to open the box." He suddenly had a desire to take a very personal interest in this case—and in Ms. Eve Shea.

Eve watched the man in the driver's seat of the Ranger Brigade cruiser out of the corner of her eye. Slender but muscular, about six feet tall, his sandy brown hair glinting silver at the temples, a few lines fanning out from his blue eyes, Commander Grant Sanderlin made her think of the sea captains she'd seen in paintings. All he needed was a peaked cap and a pipe clenched between his teeth. It was a strong, capable and yes, sexy image.

She closed her eyes and silently cursed fate or whatever had decided that now—after dozens of uninspiring dates—she met a man who lit a spark in her and he was about as unsuitable as they came. After Dane, she had sworn off dating older men. His reference to his daughters' mother alluded to divorce, but that didn't mean he hadn't remarried. And he had not one but two almost-grown daughters.

"I want to stop by your house and retrieve your safety deposit box key," he said, interrupting her thoughts. "I want to see if it really is a match to this one."

She shifted toward him in the seat. "Is that why you insisted I ride to the bank with you?"

He didn't answer, only asked, "Where do you live?"

She could have refused to tell him, but what would be the point? She had no use for that key, and the sooner this was over with, the better. She gave him the address, a rural area on the south side of town. He smiled and nodded, and her heart beat a little faster. He was a handsome man, but the fact that she was thinking about that at a time like this made her uncomfortable.

"You mentioned you used to work for the newspaper," he said. "But you own a flower shop now?"

"Yes. Eve's Garden—on Main Street."

"Am I keeping you from your work?"

Would it make a difference if she said yes? "I have an assistant who's there now." Weekday mornings were usually not particularly busy times, and Sarah was more than capable of handling anything customers were likely to need.

"You'll have to give me directions to your home," he said. "I only moved here a little over a month ago and I'm still learning my way around."

"Oh? Where did you move from?" she asked.

"Washington, DC. You might already know that the Ranger Brigade is a task force of officers from many branches of law enforcement. I'm with the FBI."

He said it the way another man might say "I'm with the post office." Or "I'm with the school district." Just another government job, though this one required him to carry a gun and arrest people.

Her gaze swept over him once more. He probably wore a shoulder holster under the suit jacket that emphasized his broad shoulders and muscular arms. He had to be at least Dane's age, but like Dane, he kept himself in shape. She supposed it was a requirement of the job.

She pulled her attention away from his body as they passed through the town of Montrose. "Turn left at the third traffic light," she said.

Her little bungalow sat in a grove of trees near the river, a rustic construction of stone and weathered metal that looked both modern and decades old. "Nice," he said, as if he meant it, as he stopped the cruiser in the driveway.

"It was built by a sculptor," she said. "I got it for a good price because it only has one bedroom and one bathroom." She took out her keys, and he followed her to the front door and waited while she unlocked it and stepped inside.

Light from the large windows spilled onto the polished wood floors and dappled the leaves of the dozens of houseplants that filled the wide windowsills. More plants, along with vases of fresh flowers, adorned the kitchen island and several side tables. "I see you like to bring your work home," the commander commented.

"I like living things in the house," she said. "And having plants is very healthy."

She stopped in the kitchen, feeling awkward. All those dates, and she hadn't invited any of those men inside her home. No one since Dane.

"The key?" he prompted.

"Oh, of course. It's back here." She indicated the short hallway that led to the bedroom, and he motioned for her to precede him.

She was acutely aware that she hadn't bothered making the bed that morning, the sheets half trailing along the floor on her side of the bed, the comforter a rumpled pile at the foot of the bed. The pajamas she'd worn—pink fleece with cartoons of sheep all over them—were draped over a white-upholstered armchair in the corner.

Aware of the man beside her taking this all in, she hurried to the dresser, and the wooden chest that served as her jewelry box. The box, of juniper wood with an inlaid marquetry hummingbird, was the work of a local artist and had been a gift from Dane their first Christmas together. That had been in the early days, when she believed they would marry and have children together.

She opened the box and lifted out the top tray, then rummaged in the loose collection of single earrings, broken bracelets, a watch that needed a battery and costume jewelry she no longer wore. "It's in here somewhere," she said.

Sanderlin came to stand beside her, the bulk and warmth of him feeling intimate in this small room, with the unmade bed just behind them. "Are you sure that's where you put it?" he asked.

"I'm positive. It was the first thing I ever put in here." She continued to rummage through the contents. "Dane gave me the box on Christmas Eve and asked me that same day to go to the bank with him to fill out the paperwork and get the key. Afterwards, we went ice skating, then had dinner and came back here and I made a point of putting the key in this box." Frustrated, she spilled the contents of the box onto the dresser. A couple of beads and some loose change spun like tops amid the tangle of necklaces, bracelets and earrings.

Sanderlin leaned closer, their shoulders rubbing, and helped her comb through the piles. "It's not here," she said.

"Are you sure you didn't give it back to Trask when you split up?" Sanderlin asked. "Maybe with a bunch of other things, and you just forgot."

"I didn't give it back," she said. "He never mentioned it, and I truly had forgotten. But I know it was here." She had a sensory memory of her fingers brushing over the toothed edge of the key as she searched for a pin to fasten a shawl only a few weeks before.

"Is anything else missing?" Sanderlin asked.

She stared at the jumble of jewelry on the dresser top, dismay growing. "Nothing. Just the key."

"Is it possible someone came in and took it?"

"You mean—broke in?" Nausea rose at the idea.

"Have you noticed anyone strange hanging around? Has anything happened to make you feel uneasy, especially in the last few days?"

"No." Could someone really have come into her home without her knowing about it?

Sanderlin glanced around the room, as if assessing the situation. "For now, let's go to the bank," he said. "We don't need your key to access the box."

Numb, she followed him out of the room. She studied the rest of the house with new eyes. Had some stranger really come in without her knowledge and stolen that key?

That was ridiculous.

"Maybe the key fell out when you were looking for something else and you didn't notice," Sanderlin said.

She nodded. "That must be it." But the skin at the back of her neck prickled. Something felt very wrong about this.

They left the house, and ten minutes later the commander pulled into the bank parking lot and followed Eve into the building. A slim young woman with jet-black hair looked up from a desk near the door. "Good morning," she said. "May I help you?"

"We need to open a safe deposit box." Sanderlin handed the woman, whose name tag identified her as Liz, the key.

Liz stood. "I'll need your identification and the box number."

"Two eight two," Eve said, and opened her wallet to her driver's license.

"You remembered," Sanderlin murmured as they followed the woman through a vault door and into a room lined on both sides with safety deposit boxes.

Was he implying she had visited the box more recently than she had told him? "Numbers tend to stick in my head," she said. She could have told him she still remembered her high school locker combination, though really, why should he care?

Liz took the key and Eve's identification to a computer terminal in one corner and began typing in information. A few seconds later, she beckoned them to her. "I'll need you to sign here, showing the date and time you're accessing the box," she said.

Eve signed the electronic keypad and Liz returned her driver's license. "I'll retrieve the box for you, and replace it when you're done."

The box felt very light when Liz handed it to Eve. "When you're ready to leave, press that button and I'll come let you out," she said, indicating a button on the wall by the vault door.

Eve waited until she and Sanderlin were alone in the vault before she carried it to the counter that ran the length of the middle of the room and lifted the top.

They both stared into the box. "It's empty," Eve said, stating the obvious. "Why would Dane send me that key when there's nothing there?"

Chapter Four

Grant pushed the button to summon a bank employee. Eve continued to examine the safety deposit box, as if she expected to find something they had missed. Her shock over finding the box empty appeared genuine, as had her consternation over being unable to find her copy of the box's key.

Liz returned. "Well, that didn't take long," she said, but her smile faded when Grant showed her his badge and identification. "I need to know who last accessed this box and when," he said.

Liz glanced from the badge to his face to the empty box. "I'll have to ask my supervisor," he said. "I believe that information is confidential."

"I have permission to access this box," Eve said. "Surely you can tell me who else has opened it."

"I'll have to ask my supervisor," Liz said again, and fled.

"Do you get that kind of reaction often?" Eve asked when they were alone again. "She acted as if she'd seen a ghost. Or maybe an ax murderer."

"The badge can catch people off guard," he said.

"Must make it tough to pick up women," she said.

"I haven't had much of a problem with that."

She turned away, but not before he caught the hint of a smile. Was she flirting with him? Because she was nervous and trying to break the tension? Or because she felt the same attraction he did?

The door to the vault opened again and a short man in a dark suit that appeared to be too large for him entered, followed by Liz. "I'm Dwight Lawson," he said. "What seems to be the problem?"

Grant displayed his badge again. "I need to know who last accessed this deposit box, and when."

"I came here today to retrieve something from the box and the box is empty," Eve said. "I want to know who else has been in here."

Lawson walked to the computer terminal and began typing. A moment later he said, "The box was opened yesterday at 4:30 p.m. by the owner, Dane Trask."

Behind Grant, Eve gasped. He reached back and squeezed her hand, a warning to let him do the talking. "Who escorted Mr. Trask into the vault?" he asked.

Lawson consulted the screen again. "Ms. Emerson is one of our senior employees," he said.

"I need to speak with her," Grant said.

"She just returned to her desk," Liz said.

"Bring her here please," Lawson said.

While Liz went to fetch her coworker, Lawson turned to Grant. "What is this about?" he asked. "I heard the news reports about Dane Trask."

"We're trying to find Mr. Trask," Grant said.

Liz returned with an attractive black woman Grant judged to be in her fifties. Her name tag identified her as Felice. She glanced at Grant and Eve, then addressed her boss. "Liz said you wanted to see me."

"You admitted a man to the vault yesterday about 4:30," Lawson said. "A Mr. Dane Trask, for box number 282."

"Yes, sir. I remember because we were going to close the lobby soon."

"What did this man look like?" Grant asked.

"Not to be rude, but who are you?" Felice asked. "I can't talk about our clients to just anyone."

"Special Agent Grant Sanderlin, with the Ranger Brigade." He showed her his badge. "We're looking for Mr. Trask."

"Don't you watch the news?" Lawson asked. "There's a $25,000 reward for information leading to Dane Trask's apprehension. The man is a suspected terrorist."

Felice's eyes widened at this, but she held her ground. "I help my daughter with my two grandsons in the evenings," she said. "The only TV I see these days is *Daniel Tiger* and *Dinosaur Train*."

"You're not in any trouble," Grant reassured her. "I just need you to describe this man for me."

She pursed her lips, considering. "He was tall," she said. "Maybe six-two. A white man, with short dark hair and brown eyes. Handsome. And very charming." She flushed, looking years younger.

Except for the eyes, that could describe Dane Trask. Or any number of other men. "You verified his identity?" he asked.

"Of course."

"What kind of identification was it?" Grant asked. "A driver's license?"

The lines on her forehead deepened. "Not a driver's license." She moved to the computer terminal and consulted the display. Her face cleared. "It was a military ID. I remember now that I thanked him for his service and he said he was happy to serve."

"I'll need to see the security feed for this area for yesterday afternoon," Grant told Lawson.

"I'll need a warrant to show you that," Lawson said.

"I can get one," Grant said.

"And while he's doing that, Dane is getting farther and farther away from us," Eve said.

Lawson looked startled, as if he had forgotten she was in the room. He turned back to Felice Emerson. "Was there anyone else in the vault area at the same time as Mr. Trask?" he asked.

"No, sir."

"Then I can show you the security footage," Lawson said. "We'll need to go into the back offices, if you're done in here."

He led the way back through the lobby, past the tellers' counter, through a door that blended in with the wall. He tapped a code on a keypad beside the door, then escorted them in, to a room where a row of wall-mounted monitors displayed black-and-white images of various areas of the bank. In the vault they had just left, Liz and Felice stood with their heads together, talking. Lawson frowned up at the image, then moved to a desk where a young man looked up from yet another monitor. "Special Agent Sanderlin is with the FBI, and he needs to see the security footage for the vault area for yesterday afternoon at 4:30."

If the man was surprised at the request, he didn't show it. His expression didn't change as he began typing, then scrolling.

"I can't believe that man was here and no one noticed," Lawson said. "That story has been all over the news."

Grant didn't answer. Eve stood at his side, silent, but practically humming with tension. He wanted to take her hand again, to steady her, but didn't think it would be appropriate.

"Here you go," the young man, who wore no name tag, said. He angled the screen toward them and they all leaned in to view a tall, dark-haired man follow Felice into the vault. He said something that made her laugh and she left him. As soon as she was gone, he opened the box, dumped the contents into the satchel he had slung over one shoulder, then summoned Felice to escort him out. The entire sequence took less than five minutes.

"He kept his head down, and angled so you can't really see his face," the young man said. "The cameras are placed to catch faces, so you'd have to make a real effort to avoid them."

The man in the video had been making an effort, even putting his hand up to shield his face at one point.

"Run it again," Grant said.

"That isn't Dane," Eve said when they had watched the clip a second time.

"I need a copy of that," Grant said. Maybe Hud could enhance the image to get a better ID.

"I don't see how you could tell who it is," Lawson said. "But Felice checked his ID. She wouldn't lie about something like that."

"IDs can be faked," Grant said.

They waited for the copy of the security feed, Grant thanked Lawson, and they left. Eve remained silent until they reached the cruiser. "That wasn't Dane," she said again.

"How can you be sure?" Grant opened the passenger door and held it for her, admiring her legs as she slid in, while trying to appear not to do so. She had very nice legs, shapely with good muscle tone.

"I just know it wasn't him." She looked pained. "We were lovers for three years. I know how he walked, how he carried himself. The person in that video—there were similarities, similar height, similar build, but that wasn't Dane."

Grant was inclined to believe her. Dane Trask's face was on posters all over town, online and on TV. The odds of him strolling into a bank at that time of day and not being recognized by anyone were slim to none.

"The shoes weren't right," Eve said.

"What do you mean?" He put the cruiser in gear and backed out of the parking space.

"The man in the photograph was wearing athletic shoes. Dane didn't even own a pair. If he needed casual shoes, he wore hiking boots or leather sandals. I used to tease him about it." Her expression was triumphant. "It definitely wasn't Dane."

"I believe you," Grant said.

"He didn't even look at the contents of the deposit box," Eve said. "He just dumped everything in that satchel."

"He was in a hurry," Grant said.

"Or maybe he didn't know exactly what he was looking for, so he took everything."

This struck Grant as particularly insightful. "That's a very good observation. Who knew Dane had given you that deposit box key?"

"No one. At least, I didn't tell anyone. And why does that matter?"

He waited, and saw when the answer came to her. Her face paled, but she held steady. "You think the person who got into that box did so with my key."

"We have Trask's key. Yours is missing."

"Someone stole the key from my house? When? And how did they know it was there?"

"A jewelry box on the bedroom dresser isn't exactly a devious hiding place," Grant said. "Experienced thieves know to check places like that."

"But again—why would anyone want to steal that key, or the contents of Dane's deposit box?"

"Maybe for the same reason Dane sent you the key. Because there was something in there he wanted the public to know about."

"Maybe whatever it was proved he isn't guilty of the crimes he's being accused of. Or maybe he put a letter in there, explaining why he disappeared." Eve hugged her arms around her middle. "How are you going to find out who's doing this and stop them?"

He couldn't decide if the question was evidence of her faith in him and his team—or an accusation. "I'll start by getting a crime scene team to go over your house. Maybe they'll find some sign of a break-in that we missed. I'll have my tech experts look at the bank security cam footage. Maybe they can enhance the image to make identifying the man in the picture easier."

"I could talk to Audra, and maybe Dane's co-workers," Eve said. "Maybe one of them knows something."

"No." He didn't wait for her reaction, merely closed the space between them and took her hand. "Whoever did this, they could be dangerous. You need to go about your regular life and let me handle this. If anyone is watching you, let them believe you don't even know the key is missing. Don't get involved."

"What do you mean, if someone is watching me?" Instead of pulling away, she leaned into him. "If you're saying that just to frighten me, it's working."

He forced himself to release his hold on her. It was either that or pull her close and kiss that terrified look away. But that kind of he-man behavior had never been his style, so he took a step back, and kept his expression neutral and professional. He slid a business card from his pocket and handed it to her. "If you see anyone suspicious, or if anything happens to make you feel uncomfortable or uneasy, you call me. Anytime, day or night."

She stared at the card. "Do you think I'm in danger?"

He wanted to reassure her that she would be fine, that he would never let anyone harm her, and there was no need for her to worry. But he respected her too much to lie to her. "You're probably fine," he said. "But I like to exercise what we call an abundance of caution. You don't have to change anything you're doing now, just be aware and report anything suspicious."

She compressed her lips together and nodded, then tucked his card into her purse. "Does this mean I'm going to see you again?" she asked.

The question caught him off guard. For a flash of an instant, his all-business demeanor slipped and he stared at her. "Would you like that?"

She very deliberately looked him up and down, that ghost of a smile playing about her full lips again. "If I am in danger, you look like a handy man to have around, that's all."

He knew a challenge when he heard one—and he was more than ready to meet this one. "I plan on sticking close," he said. He'd leave it up to her how close he could get, but the next few weeks—or months, or maybe even years—with her could prove very interesting.

Chapter Five

"There you are. I was beginning to think you'd been arrested." Sarah greeted Eve from behind the wire frame of an archway she was filling with greenery and fresh flowers when Eve returned to the flower shop that afternoon.

"Sorry I was gone so long." Eve stashed her purse under the counter and moved in to help trim the rose-buds, baby's breath and tree fern Sarah was inserting into test tube vases and wiring to the arch.

"What happened?" Sarah asked. She didn't stop working, but she fixed Eve with an expectant gaze.

"I ended up speaking to the Ranger Brigade commander." Sarah clipped a broken stem from a branch of baby's breath, then began separating the branch into smaller pieces.

"Oh? What was he like?"

"He was...nice." Less prickly and much kinder than she had expected. She had thought he would view Dane as a criminal and her as bad by association, and possibly even an accomplice. Instead, he'd been sympathetic. Even understanding, if a little too nosy for her comfort.

"Nice?" Sarah set aside the coil of florist's wire and turned to face Eve, hands on hips. "Nice how? Nice charming? Nice looking?"

"Both, I guess." Eve poked a stem of fern into one of the test tubes and added a rosebud. *Powerful. Sexy.*

"You're blushing!" Sarah chuckled. "Oh, this has got to be good. Tell me everything. Are you going to go out with him?"

"What? No!" She gave up on the flowers and set them aside. "I went there to turn over the stuff Dane sent me, not to get a date." But she'd flirted with him. She hadn't been able to stop herself.

"You're clearly attracted to this guy. I haven't seen you blush over anyone in months. And the plan was you would go out with anyone eligible." Sarah's smile faded. "Or is he not eligible?"

"He's even older than Dane and he has two teenage daughters."

"So he's married."

"Divorced. But he's older, with older children. Like Dane."

"So you're attracted to more mature men." Sarah elbowed her. "Nothing wrong with that."

"Sarah, I'm not going to date this man. I mean, he

could end up arresting Dane, and that would be…" She let her voice trail away.

"Yeah, awkward." Sarah picked up the wire and clippers once more. "So what happened?"

"I gave him the letter and he insisted on driving me to my house to retrieve the safety deposit box key Dane gave me that first year we were dating."

"I guess he wanted to see if it was a match," Sarah said.

"I think he didn't want me opening the box and taking out anything incriminating before he had a chance to see it."

"You wouldn't do that," Sarah said. "Would you?"

"Of course I wouldn't."

"Not in your right mind, of course, but love messes with people's minds."

"I'm not in love with Dane anymore." That was true. She had cared deeply about him at one time, but over the last six months of their relationship, and in the six months since they had broken up, she had come to see him in a different light. He was a good man, but he kept his emotions too tightly controlled. She needed a man who was able to show her love more, the kind of man who could be silly with a child or sentimental with her. He didn't have to be just like her, he merely had to be willing to meet her halfway when it came to expressing his feelings.

"Okay, so you got the key from your house," Sarah said. "Then what?"

"We didn't get the key. It wasn't there."

"You mean you couldn't find it. Couldn't you remember where you put it?"

"I knew I put it in the jewelry box on my dresser. But it wasn't there."

"Maybe you just forgot, or—"

"I didn't forget. The commander thinks someone broke into my place and took it."

"Someone broke into your place? When?" Sarah put an arm around Eve's shoulders. "Oh honey, that's so awful. What else did they take?"

"They didn't take anything else, except the key. And they didn't do any damage. I wouldn't have suspected anything if not for that missing key."

"But—"

"Don't interrupt, just listen."

Sarah covered her lips with one hand and nodded, eyes wide.

Eve told her about going to the bank and discovering someone had been there before them—someone who claimed to be Dane Trask. "I watched the security camera footage," Eve said. "The man was similar to Dane, but it wasn't Dane. And he had a key to get into the deposit box. I have Dane's key, so this impersonator must have had mine."

"Or he obtained another key somehow."

"The bank only issues two. If you lose one, you have to pay a couple hundred dollars to have the lock drilled out and replaced."

"Huh." Sarah clipped a foot-long length of wire and wrapped one end twice around the neck of a flower-filled test tube. "If it wasn't Dane, who was it?"

"I don't know. That's what the commander and his officers are trying to find out." She picked up the clippers again and snipped at a cluster of miniature roses. The tension of the day had drained her. All she wanted to do was go home, take a hot shower and go to bed. Alone.

Liar, her conscience whispered. She wanted to go home to a man who loved her, one who would hold her and comfort her and declare his intention to slay dragons if need be to console her.

"Oh, I almost forgot." Sarah patted Eve's shoulder. "A man stopped by to see you just before lunch. A really good-looking guy. Early thirties, nice suit, no wedding ring." Sarah ticked off these points like a bird-watcher listing the identifying features of a rare avian find. Eve knew the genus and species of this particular rarity by heart. Where she was concerned, at least, hominid eligible—the eligible man—was a rare find indeed.

"What was his name?" Eve asked. "Did he say why he wanted to see me?" Maybe one of the men she had met online decided to come meet her in person—a scary thought, given that information about where she lived and worked was supposed to be kept confidential.

"He just said he had been hoping to meet you. He asked if he could leave his card on your desk. I was busy putting this thing together." Sarah indicated the arch. "So I said yes. Then I forgot about it until just now."

Eve squeezed around Sarah and headed for her office. She spotted the business card while she was still in the hall, a small rectangle of white card stock in the center of her desk blotter. Her mysterious visitor hadn't tossed the card onto the desk. He had place it precisely in the center of the desktop.

"So, who was he?" Sarah crowded into the doorway beside Eve. "Did he say what he wanted?"

Eve leaned forward and plucked the card from the blotter. "Toby Masterson," she read. Her heart beat harder as the smaller print under his name registered. "He's an accountant with TDC Enterprises." The company Dane had worked for.

The company that had accused him of serious crimes.

"Is there a note?" Sarah asked.

Eve flipped the card over. This side was blank. "Did he say anything else you haven't told me?" she asked.

"No, I swear." Sarah actually crossed herself. "But he seemed really nice. Very friendly."

Sarah made friends with everyone. She had a knack for getting a smile or at least a pleasant word out of the surliest customers. But just because Mr.

Masterson succumbed to Sarah's charm didn't mean he was a nice person. "Did he say anything else?" she asked.

"Only that he'd stop by again some time." Sarah's smile broadened. "Just think, you might have two handsome men pursuing you. Wouldn't that be a nice change?"

"I don't want to be pursued." Especially by a man she'd never met who sought her out. She frowned at his card again. Was it possible she had met him, and had forgotten? She shook her head and tucked the card in her desk drawer. She didn't have time to fret over Mr. Masterson. She had work to do. "You can go home as soon as you're done with that arch," she told Sarah. "I'll close up the shop. I'll probably stay late, working on the order for the Salazar wedding."

"Thanks. I was going to ask if I could leave early. Robby is having a mini meltdown over having to pick out a tux for prom at the end of next month. I promised I'd help him out."

Eve tried to imagine Sarah's youngest child, who at sixteen was already six-foot-four-inches and probably weighed all of 120 pounds, in a tuxedo, and failed. Did they even make formal wear with legs that long? "Good luck," she said. "If you need to leave now, I can finish the arch."

"I'm almost done. Manuel promised he'd be by a little before five to pick it up to deliver to the Elks

Hall for some kind of ceremony they're having tonight."

Eve settled in to work and was soon absorbed in planning arrangements, calculating flower totals and filling out order forms. Sarah left and Manuel came and went. At six o'clock she switched off the lights in the front room, locked the door and turned the sign to Closed, then returned to her desk. She was on her way back to her desk when her cell phone rang, with a call from Cara Mead, Dane's administrative assistant.

"Cara! What is it? Have you heard something about Dane?" Eve answered.

"Not a thing," Cara said. "When he does surface again, I'm going to give him what-for for worrying us all so much."

Eve pictured the petite brown-haired Cara standing on tiptoe to grab the six-two Dane by the ear to pull him down to her level. "I suppose you've seen those horrible reward posters around town," she said. "When I spotted one in the post office this morning, I felt a little sick. I just can't believe Dane would do the things he's accused of."

"I don't believe it either," Cara said. "I think someone is trying to cover up something and making Dane the scapegoat. That's sort of why I'm calling."

"Oh?" Eve sank into her desk chair once more, the flower order forgotten.

"I'm not working with TDC anymore," Cara said.

"With Dane gone, it was pretty clear they wanted me out of the way, too. I have a new job, as coordinator for Wilderness Conservation."

"Congratulations." Eve tried to put some enthusiasm behind the words, but this news pained her. Had Cara left her job because she didn't believe Dane was coming back? "That must be interesting work."

"It is. And one of the first things on my agenda when I took on the position was looking into the Mary Lee Mine site. It was one of the last projects Dane worked on and I think he found something wrong up there. I was able to send in some soil and water samples for testing and they came back way out of whack. My group is trying to pressure TDC to do more testing, and to take responsibility for the test results. We're holding a rally and a press conference at the mine tomorrow and I was hoping you'd agree to be there."

"Me? Cara, that really isn't my thing."

"The more people we have present, the bigger impact we'll make, and the more pressure we'll put on TDC," Cara said. "I really think this is what Dane would want us to do. Please? It won't take much of your time."

Eve wavered. She had plenty of work here at the shop, but it wasn't anything Sarah couldn't handle. "I'll think about it," she hedged.

"We're meeting at the grocery store parking lot at

eight to drive up to the mine," Cara said. "I'd really, really appreciate it if you could be there."

Eve ended the call and her chair creaked as she leaned back. With her love of flowers and plants, environmental activism seemed a good fit. But she had never been one to make waves or put herself in the spotlight. She preferred to sit back and enjoy the flowers.

She had to admit that if people didn't speak out to protect the environment, how long would it be before the flowers she loved disappeared altogether? She could almost hear Dane asking the question. He had a way of puncturing her fantasy balloons with practical reality.

Still, they had had a lot of good times together. She recalled an outing where they had visited a lavender farm. A farm worker had taken a photo of her and Dane sitting in a field of lavender, all smiles. It was one of her favorite photos and even after they had broken up, she hadn't been able to bring herself to put it away.

Her gaze roamed over the office. The small space didn't have room for much in the way of personalization or decoration, but she had managed to squeeze in a small bookcase, which she filled with a few figurines and pictures that were meaningful to her, including the lavender fields photograph. She scanned the shelves and realized with a jolt it wasn't there.

The space it usually occupied, second shelf down, all the way over to the right, was empty.

Had Sarah moved it for some reason? No, she wouldn't do something like that. Had someone else taken it, then?

But why? Who would want a picture of her and Dane together?

Fear chilled her. Anxious not to be alone one moment longer, she collected her sweater and purse, and left via the rear entrance. She felt better once she was outside. Plenty of people were out and about this early in the evening: shoppers, diners, other people headed home from work. She waved to a couple she knew and forced herself to walk calmly to her car. She thought about calling the commander to tell him about the missing picture, but quickly discarded the idea. He'd think she was a nut. First she couldn't find the safe deposit key. Now she had misplaced a photograph. And who kept a photograph of a man she broke up with six months ago?

There was probably a good explanation for all of this. She should have looked behind the shelf. Maybe the picture had merely fallen down. Or maybe Sarah did have it. She'd find out tomorrow. Meanwhile, she was going to go home and not think about it. Ignoring problems might not make them vanish, but sometimes it was the best coping mechanism. If only everything in life could be dealt with so simply.

Chapter Six

Tuesday morning, Grant dialed his ex-wife's number and waited for the phone to ring. He would have preferred to call his daughters directly, but he had learned the hard way that they both seldom answered. He could have texted, but communicating that way wasn't the same as hearing his girls' voices. Since they were both on spring break, he hoped by calling early he would find them at home.

"Hello." Angela's voice was cool and professional—her telephone voice. Caller ID would have shown her the call was from him, but she always answered as if speaking to a stranger. Perhaps that's what they had become, in the end.

"Hello, Angela," he said. "Are the girls around? I'd like to speak to them." No small talk, asking how she was doing or what was new in her life. She refused to respond, so he'd given up.

"I'll see if they're available." As if they were busy executives, not teenagers.

"Hey, Daddy!" Janie's greeting made his heart lift. He pictured her, smile full of braces, red-gold hair in a wild tangle, hazel eyes sparkling. "When are you coming to visit?" she asked. "I've missed you so much."

"I've missed you, too, Pumpkin," he said. He ignored her question about a visit. Taking any kind of leave from a job he had just started was out of the question, but work had kept him away from them all their lives, and he hated repeating himself. One day, when they were adults with jobs and responsibilities, maybe they'd understand. "What have you been up to?"

"I got an A on my English paper about subversive feminism in *Jane Eyre*," she said.

"That's great." Though what in the world a sophomore was doing writing about something like that he didn't know. Janie was scary smart sometimes. "Did you get the packet of stuff I sent you?"

"I did! The park looks so interesting. Like the real Wild West. I can't wait to see it."

"This summer," he said. As much as he looked forward to the girls spending two months with him, he worried they'd be bored within a week. Montrose, Colorado, didn't offer the social opportunities of Washington, DC. But he'd do his best to make the visit worthwhile.

"I don't want to wait until then," Janie said.

"It's only another couple of months," he said. "In

the meantime, look over the stuff I sent you and think about everything you want to do and see while you're here."

"I will."

"Can I talk to your sister now?"

"Beth is being a pain right now. Don't take it personally." Translation: Beth was still refusing to talk to him because, as she had said in their last heated exchange before he left, it was bad enough that he'd been gone all the time while they were growing up. Now he was moving thousands of miles away without even considering them.

The words hurt more than any bullet. All he could do was keep the lines open and hope that one day she would talk to him again. "Tell her I said hello and I love her," he said. "And I love you, too."

"I love you, Daddy," Janie said. "And Mom says I have to get off the phone now because we're going sailing with some friends of Darryl's, which will probably be really boring. Goodbye!"

She ended the call and he laid down the phone. Darryl was Angela's new husband, a lobbyist who had set Grant's teeth on edge every time they met. This was the man he had abandoned his family to.

Walk it back, he silently chided himself. No good came of wallowing. He turned his attention to the next item on his lengthy to-do list. The background check he'd ordered on Eve Shea.

No criminal record. Not even a speeding ticket.

Her business, Eve's Garden, had a good reputation and appeared to be making a reasonable profit. No marriages. No bankruptcy. In her time as a reporter with the *Montrose Daily Press*, she had won two Press Association awards.

He closed the report and swiveled away from the monitor. He had no reason to believe Eve was faking her lack of knowledge about what had happened to the contents of the safe deposit box, but he had to be sure. For the integrity of the case and for his personal integrity, he needed to know he hadn't let his attraction to her interfere with him carrying out his duties.

His intercom beeped. "Yes?"

Faith Martin's voice answered. "Sir, we've had a request for assistance from the Montrose County Sheriff's Department. They'd like our help with crowd control at the Mary Lee Mine."

"What's going on up there?" he asked. Hazardous waste remediation at the Mary Lee was one of the projects Dane Trask had been working on when he disappeared. More recently, Officer Jason Beck and Trask's administrative assistant, Cara Mead, had been attacked when they tried to investigate the mine site. And of course, the mine had been the focus of the press release someone—presumably Trask—had sent to Eve.

"Some protesters are holding a press conference there this morning, and MCSD is concerned there might be trouble. And since the mine is in the Ranger Brigade's jurisdiction, they thought we could help."

"The mine is private property within the public lands we monitor," Grant clarified. "But yes, we can help. Who's in this morning?"

"Lieutenant Dance is here, and Officer Hudson."

"Thanks."

Grant pulled on a black windbreaker against the late spring chill and went in search of Dance.

Lieutenant Dance looked up from his computer keyboard at the commander's approach. One look at Grant's face and he sat up straighter. "Something's up?" he asked.

"You and I are helping with crowd control for a press conference at the Mary Lee Mine."

Dance unfolded his muscular frame and pulled on his own windbreaker. "You drive," Grant said. Dance knew the location of the mine better than he did.

Whether or not there was trouble at the mine, it was a beautiful day to be driving backroads in the wilderness. Hillsides glowed a soft pink with wild crocus, and aspens unfurled lime green leaves like splashes of Day-Glo paint against the more somber hues of pinion and fir. A hawk traced wide circles across an expanse of turquoise sky unmarred by even a single cloud.

"I saw a poster about this meeting at the coffee shop this morning," Dance said as he turned the cruiser off the highway and up a jagged dirt road.

"Something about a press conference to bring to light TDC's failure to address matters of grave environmental concern."

Grant nodded. "Words most likely to get TDC Enterprises and their lawyers riled."

"Riled enough to cause trouble?" Dance asked.

"Not physical trouble," Grant said. "I think they'd be more likely to employ their lawyers to send letters threatening legal action and expensive lawsuits."

Dance nodded. "So maybe we'll have a nice couple hours in the mountains." He gunned the vehicle up a steep washed-out section of road. "Maybe without a lot of company. Not many people will want to risk their cars on this road."

But when they arrived at the mine gates, Grant was surprised to see at least two dozen cars and vans, and he estimated more than fifty people gathered around a wooden platform constructed of pallets. A couple of people held shoulder-mounted television cameras, while others carried microphones and recording equipment.

A quartet of stern-faced men and women in suits stood to one side of the platform, scowling at the growing crowd. Probably the lawyers, Grant thought, as he strode past a cluster of people who carried signs that read TDC Pollutes and Don't Let Corporate Greed Destroy the Future.

He faltered and did a double take as he recognized the woman who held the latter sign. Eve Shea met his gaze and lifted her chin in a defiant gesture.

He veered off course and walked over to her. "Hello, Ms. Shea," he said.

"You might as well call me Eve," she said, lowering the sign.

"Are you a member of Wilderness Conservation?" he asked.

"No. Cara Mead asked me to come. She's the coordinator for Wilderness Conservation now."

And Cara—his officer, Jason Beck's fiancée—had been the one to discover that TDC's supposed efforts to clean up the old mine site had, so far at least, resulted in even more contamination at the site, contrary to what was shown in the reports TDC had filed with the Environmental Protection Agency and others.

So maybe TDC had fudged their data, or even outright lied, but Grant wasn't sure that made them dangerous.

"Why are you here, Commander?" Eve asked.

"We're here in case anything gets out of hand," he said.

She pushed a wayward strand of hair out of her face. "It's a press conference."

"And a protest." He indicated her sign.

She looked down at the sign. "Someone handed me this when we got here. I think it's mainly to give the news cameras an interesting visual."

She made an interesting visual, he thought, the wind lifting strands of her hair to float around her like a veil, her cheeks flushed from either sun or emotion, a soft blue tunic over black leggings and boots clinging to her curves. "I was going to call you today and let you know my investigators didn't find any signs that your locks were forced," he said.

"I didn't think so, but I guess it's good to have it confirmed," she said. "Maybe I really did misplace that deposit box key."

"A good set of lock picks or a key could have opened your door without leaving behind any evidence," Grant said. "Did you find anything else missing?"

"Not from my home, no."

Something in her voice or her facial expression alerted him. "Did you find something missing from somewhere else? Your shop?"

"It's probably nothing," she said.

"What is it?"

"I had a picture of myself and Dane, in a field of lavender. For years it has sat on a shelf in my office. Now it's not there."

"When was the last time you saw it?" he asked.

She shook her head. "I have no idea. It's one of those things that has been there so long I don't really even notice it anymore."

"When did you notice it was missing?"

"Yesterday evening. I was finishing up work for

the day and looked over, and realized the spot where it usually sat was empty."

"Could it have fallen behind the shelf, or been moved?"

"I looked this morning, but I couldn't find it." She shrugged. "I'm sure it's somewhere. I mean, who would steal a photograph?"

"Hello, everyone." The voice, overly loud in the speakers that had been erected on either end of the platform, was jarring. Cara Mead, all five-foot-three of her, in black trousers and a purple jacket, leaned back from the mic and tried again. "We're so glad you could join us on this beautiful day in this beautiful place."

Grant wasn't sure he would have termed the piles of gray rock and old building materials that formed the backdrop of this scene as beautiful, but it had a certain untamed appeal. "As you may already be aware, TDC Industries accepted a contract last August to mitigate contaminants at the Mary Lee Mine, removing or quarantining harmful substances like mercury and arsenic, and returning this place to its natural beauty. Instead, recent test results show there are actually more of some contaminants than before."

"Eve Shea, this is a pleasure."

Grant and Eve both turned to look at the man who had spoken. Taller than Grant by at least two inches, he had the sharp features and deep tan of a man who spent a lot of time outdoors.

"Toby Masterson." He offered his hand to Eve, ignoring Grant.

"My assistant said you stopped by my shop while I was out yesterday," Eve said. She shook hands, but immediately afterwards folded her arms tight across her chest.

"I was disappointed not to hear from you," Masterson said.

"I've been busy. And since I don't know you…" She shrugged.

"But you know Dane Trask. And I'm looking for him. I think you could help." He rested his hand on her shoulder and squeezed. Eve grimaced.

"Why are you looking for Dane?" Grant asked. He wanted to tell the man to take his hands off Eve, but sensed she might resist that approach.

Sure enough, Eve took care of the matter herself, shoving Masterson's hand away. She moved over, putting more distance between them. "If Dane wants to stay away he must have his reasons," she said. "I won't help anyone find him."

She looked at Grant, not Masterson, when she spoke, and he felt again that spark of desire, almost painful in its intensity.

"Still, I'd love to get together and talk," Masterson said.

"I don't have anything to say to you." She started to turn away, but Masterson moved to block her.

"Then listen to me," he said. "I knew Dane Trask from Welcome Home Warriors. He could be a great guy, and he did a lot of good work. But he had a dark side, too. He could be really dangerous. I think he could be dangerous to you."

Eve's face blanched china white, and she put a hand to her throat. "Dane would never hurt me," she said.

"You hurt him," Masterson said. "He was going to ask you to marry him and instead you dumped him."

"He understood. We weren't right for each other."

"He was an expert at hiding his emotions. You know that." He took a step back. "Take my advice and be careful. And don't think you need to protect him from anyone. Worry about protecting yourself."

He turned and left them, shoving through the crowd of reporters and onlookers, until Grant couldn't see him anymore.

Grant moved closer to Eve. "Are you all right?" he asked.

She took a deep breath. "I'm okay." She stared after Masterson. "I didn't like him."

"Neither do I. But maybe you should listen to him."

She glared at him. "What do you mean?"

"We don't know why Dane did what he did—why he left his job and the people who cared about him to hide out in the wilderness. Why he wrecked a really nice truck or sent you that cryptic letter. But one explanation is that those aren't the actions of a mentally stable man. Maybe something happened to change him. To trigger him."

She shook her head, but he slid his hand up to cradle her cheek, stilling her. "Maybe Dane is dangerous," he said. "Maybe you do need to be careful, and stay as far away from him as you can."

"Since he isn't here, that shouldn't be a problem," she said.

"I should have said I think it would be better if you stayed away from anything to do with Trask— like that safety deposit box, or this rally."

She pulled away, color rising in her cheeks. "I don't like people telling me what to do," she said. "And I really don't respond well to scare tactics." She raised the sign again, as if prepared to use it as a weapon, then turned her back on him.

Grant stepped away, stung a little, but continued to watch her.

Toby Masterson had his eyes on Eve, too, and the look on his face had made Grant want to punch the man. Was that his cop sense at work—or plain old-fashioned jealousy?

Chapter Seven

"I'm sure that picture of you and Dane was in your office on Monday morning," Sarah said when Eve asked her about it Tuesday afternoon. "We had a slow spell and I tidied up a little bit and dusted your bookcase."

"And you're sure the picture was there?" Eve asked.

Sarah nodded. "I'm sure because I wondered why you kept it out, since the two of you weren't a couple anymore."

"I kept it out because I really like the photograph." Eve glared. "Dane and I are still friends, even if we aren't lovers."

Sarah held up both hands in a defensive gesture. "All right, all right. I just worry that if you aren't really over him, you'll never make room in your life for someone else."

"What self-help book did you get that out of?" Eve asked.

Sarah grinned. "I could write the self-help book

on that one. I've raised three girls and a boy who are constantly falling in and out love."

"What's the latest with Robby?" Eve asked, glad for a switch in subject.

"Let's look for that photograph and I'll tell you all about it."

While the two women moved furniture and looked everywhere they could think of for the missing photograph, Sarah regaled Eve with a description of the previous day's outing to find the perfect tuxedo for prom. "You know Robby," she said. "He wanted something different, but not too different. He wants to stand out, but not too far out."

"In other words, he's a typical teenager." Eve yanked open a file drawer and stared at the paperwork shoved in so tightly there was no way the picture could be inside. "What did he end up with?"

"He went with a pretty traditional black tux, dressed up with a purple-and-gold paisley vest and a white ascot. Sort of the Regency fop look—though when I said that, he had no idea what I was talking about, which led to a discussion of Jane Austen, Georgette Heyer, and my love of Regency romance novels that had him rolling his eyes. But he seemed satisfied when I told him the girls were bound to find him irresistible."

Eve sank into her desk chair. "Tell him when he's ready for the big day, whatever flowers he wants are on the house. I don't think we're going to find that picture. It's just disappeared."

"I'm sorry," Sarah said. "Are you really upset?"

Was she? "I did like the picture, but I'm more upset by the idea that someone may have come into my office and taken it. Why would anyone even want it?"

"It's a mystery, all right." Sarah leaned back against the door frame. "But maybe you'll meet someone soon whose picture you'll want to put in its place."

At Eve's sour look, she laughed. "I can't help it if I'm a hopeless romantic. I want to see you happy."

Eve sat up straighter. "I don't need a man to be happy."

"No, but you do need a man to make a baby, and I know how much you want to be a mother."

"Maybe I'll find a sperm donor." Even as she said the words, her throat tightened in fear. Sure, women did a wonderful job raising children on their own every day, either out of necessity or by choice, but did she really want to do that? Maybe she was old-fashioned, but she had a hard time letting go of her dreams of a happy family—a child or children and two parents.

"Who are you going out with this weekend?" Sarah asked.

"I'm thinking of taking a break." She focused on her computer screen, hoping Sarah would get the message that she didn't want to talk about it.

But her friend wasn't so easily deterred. "Don't tell me you're giving up so soon."

"Maybe this isn't the way to go about it," Eve said. "I don't seem to be hitting it off with any of the men I've dated, or else they're not interested in me."

"What about that professor from the university?" Sarah asked. "I always thought the two of you had a lot in common."

"He told me—to my face—that he preferred younger women. I took it to mean he usually dated his students."

"Ewww." Sarah wrinkled her nose. "Okay, well, what about the insurance salesman?"

"He tried to sell me a life insurance policy on our first date. I don't know, it just set the wrong tone. Then there was the man who spent most of the date on the phone with his ex-girlfriend. Or the guy who brought his dog along on the date."

"You like dogs."

"I love dogs. But this one sat between us the whole time and growled at me. At the end of the evening the man told me things weren't going to work out between us because his dog obviously didn't like me."

"What is wrong with men?" Sarah asked.

"Maybe I'm being too picky," Eve said.

"No," Sarah said. "You want what you want, and it isn't these guys." She sighed. "You and Dane were good together—until you weren't."

"Dane and I are never getting back together," Eve protested.

"No, hear me out," Sarah said. She straightened. "You don't want or need Dane anymore, I agree, but maybe he's your type, so you need to find someone like him—only better. A good-looking, mature man who wants a family. An athletic, outdoorsy type. Maybe former military."

"I don't know. Does such a guy even exist?"

"Face it, that's what you were attracted to. It's why you're attracted to that police commander with the Ranger Brigade."

"He's FBI," Sarah corrected her. "And I already told you he isn't right for me. He already has two almost grown daughters."

"That doesn't mean he doesn't want more children. Maybe he loves children. Maybe he's secretly longing to find the right woman to raise more children with."

"Maybe he's a great cook and loves to clean house, too," Eve said. "I mean, as long as we're fantasizing about the perfect man, let's go all the way."

"He doesn't have to be perfect," Sarah said. "He just has to be perfect for you. There's someone out there for you, I know there is."

"I wish I had your faith." Eve straightened. "Now come on, we both have work to do. We'd better make sure we have plenty of supplies for corsages, wristlets, hair clips and boutonnieres," she said. "Lots of carnations and baby roses and ribbon."

"I'll get right on it."

After Sarah left, Eve tried to concentrate on proofing the order for the Salazar wedding. But Sarah's words kept echoing in her head. Was it true she had a type of man she was drawn to? But what if her type was all wrong?

She sent in the order form for the wedding, then called the wedding photographer and discussed getting some shots of the bouquets and table arrangements to use in her portfolio and possibly in future advertising. She put together a Get Well Soon arrangement for a woman who broke her arm in a climbing accident, then returned to her computer to get the contact information for the head of a local charity for whom they had supplied flowers for a fundraising banquet, to see if she needed more flowers this year.

She was engrossed in plans for a new summer sales flyer when the front buzzer sounded. "Hello? May I help you?" Sarah asked.

"I'd like to speak to Eve. Ms. Shea."

The voice was unmistakable. Eve rolled her chair back a few inches and looked out at Grant Sanderlin. He wasn't in uniform, or a suit, but dressed casually in dark jeans and a polo shirt.

"Oh, Eve!" Sarah practically sang the words.

Sarah stood, smoothed her slacks and walked out to greet him. "Hello, Commander," she said.

"I'm not in uniform. Why don't you call me Grant?"

Aware of Sarah watching them while pretending to sort greeting cards at the stand in the corner, Eve struggled to keep her expression smooth. "What can I do for you?" she asked.

"I did a little checking into Toby Masterson's background," he said. "I thought you'd be interested in what I learned."

"Why were you looking into his background?" she asked. "Is he a suspect in a crime?"

"I didn't like the way he approached you at the rally this morning. And I could tell he made you uncomfortable. You have good instincts, I think."

Sarah had stopped trying to hide her interest and was watching them openly now. "Maybe we should talk about this outside," Eve said.

"It's almost time for you to close," he said. "Maybe we could discuss this over dinner."

"I don't know…" she began.

"What a great idea." Sarah rushed forward. "I can close up here. You go ahead." She nudged Eve toward her office. "He's your type," she whispered, Eve hoped softly enough that Grant didn't hear.

Eve relented. Having dinner with Commander Sanderlin probably wasn't the worst way to spend an evening, and she was curious to hear what he had learned about Toby Masterson. "I'll just get my jacket and purse," she said, and slipped into her office.

While she was fishing her purse out of the desk drawer, she heard Sarah ask, "Were you ever in the military?"

"I served ten years in the air force," Grant said.

"I knew it. You just have that look about you."

Eve rushed to rejoin them before Sarah could ask any more probing questions. "I'm ready," she said, already moving toward the door.

On the sidewalk, Grant touched her elbow. "Where are you rushing off to?" he asked.

She forced herself to slow. "I was just anxious to get out of there before Sarah started grilling you like an overprotective parent. She's a great friend, but she can't get away from trying to, I don't know, mother me."

He smiled, an expression that transformed his face to such arresting handsomeness she felt warm clear to her toes. She looked away, afraid at any moment her mouth would drop open and she'd assume the vacant, adoring look of a smitten teen. That would be beyond mortifying. "Do you need to get your car?" he asked.

"I left my car at home and walked to work after the rally this morning," she said. "Parking can get very congested downtown and I figure I need the exercise."

"Where would you like to go for dinner?"

"There's a good Himalayan restaurant at the end of the block," she said.

"That sounds good."

The owner's wife greeted them at the door and, instead of seating them at one of the tables in the front room, led them to a secluded booth in the back of the restaurant. Did they really look so much like a couple on a date? Eve wondered.

"This is good," Grant said, sliding into the booth across from her. "It's quiet, so we can talk."

"Tell me about Toby Masterson," Eve said.

"Let's order first."

They decided on an assortment of small plates and hot tea. Eve leaned back in her seat and cradled a cup of tea. "Well?"

"Toby Masterson really does know Dane Trask from Welcome Home Warriors, the veteran's organization Dane founded."

"Dane was very proud of the work WHW did to help veterans reintegrate into society," Eve said. "He worked very hard at it. But I never saw any sign that he was unbalanced, as Masterson claimed this morning. And he never acted particularly upset over us splitting up. He accepted it was never going to work out between us."

"Why was that?" Grant asked. "Why were you both so certain the relationship wouldn't work? After all, hadn't you been together three years?"

She stared into the teacup. Would it really matter

if she told this man the truth? "I very much would like to have children," she said. "Dane wasn't interested. He helped raise his daughter, Audra, and he said he was done. He was very firm about that. If I wanted to stay with him, I'd have to give up my dreams of raising children and I wasn't willing to do that." She met his gaze. "I'm not willing to do that."

He nodded, his expression unreadable. At least he didn't express sympathy with Dane's position. "I never found any evidence of violent or unlawful behavior when I checked into Trask's background," he said. "I can't say the same for Masterson."

"What did you find?"

"Domestic violence charges on two occasions. That was two years ago, when he was first discharged from the army. He's had a clean record since them and took the job with TDC three months ago. Apparently, Trask recommended him for the position."

She sipped her tea. "That sounds like something Dane would do," she said. "He was always trying to find jobs for his guys—that's what he called the men and women who came to WHW for help." She set aside her cup and leaned across the table toward him. "That's another reason I don't think Dane just ran away on a whim. He felt a real sense of responsibility to the people in Welcome Home Warriors. He wouldn't run away and leave them in the lurch. If he left, it must have been because he felt he had no choice."

"Then why doesn't he come forward now and tell us his reasons?" There was no missing the annoyance in Grant's voice. "Why the mysterious messages and inflammatory press releases and other games?"

"I don't know," she said. "I wish I did."

A server delivered their meal, and they passed the next few minutes filling their plates from the various dishes. "This is very good," Grant said after the first few bites. "It's been a long time since I had Himalayan food."

"We have a lot of good restaurants for such a small town," she said. "Though probably not the variety you're used to in DC."

"It's nice to have someone to eat with," he said.

The warmth in his tone touched her. He really was a nice man. It wasn't his fault she was so conflicted over her relationship possibilities. "It is," she agreed.

"Tell me about your flower shop," he said. "How did you get started? I'm not asking as a cop, just because I'm interested."

She told him how she had started working part-time for another flower shop while she was still a reporter. "I was getting burned out on the job at the paper," she said. "The long hours and the horrible pay. The abuse you take from the people you're reporting on and sometimes from the readers, too. I was looking for something new and discovered I had a talent for growing plants and arranging flowers. And a good head for the business side, too. I took a few courses, and when the owner of the shop announced she was retiring, I wrote a business plan, got a small business loan, and turned in my resignation to the paper."

"You took a big risk."

"I've always believed if you weren't happy in your life, then it was up to you to take action to change it." It was why she had broken up with Dane. Why she was considering different ways to have the children she wanted so much. "I figured if things didn't work out, I could always find another job," she said. "Fortunately, things worked out. What about you? How did you end up with the FBI?"

"I worked in military intelligence. When I was discharged, the CIA recruited me, but I wanted to stick with the domestic side of law enforcement, which meant the FBI."

She savored a bite of saag paneer. "Do you like the work?"

"I don't like the politics, but every job has that, to some extent. I like working on cases, and putting some really bad people behind bars. It's important work and I have a talent for it."

He spoke matter-of-factly, not bragging, but not assuming false humility. "And now you're a commander," she said.

"It's different, since my team is made up of men and women from lots of different branches of law enforcement. But we're on our own out here, with a certain degree of independence that allows us to do our job without a lot of bureaucratic interference."

"You get to run the show the way you want." That was one of the things she appreciated about having her own business.

"More or less."

They finished the meal in companionable silence. When she looked up from her plate, she invariably found his eyes on her, but the knowledge didn't make her uncomfortable. When they had eaten their fill and were finishing the last of the tea, she turned her thoughts back to the information he had shared earlier. "If Toby Masterson approaches me again, should I talk to him about Dane?" she asked.

"That's up to you," Grant said. "But I wouldn't recommend engaging with the guy."

"Why did he even seek me out? What does he have to gain from that?"

"A place in the limelight. Or maybe he just wants to get your attention."

She laughed. "Telling me my old boyfriend is dangerous isn't the best pickup line I've ever heard. It could be the worst."

"He's probably harmless," Grant said. "But if he gives you any trouble, let me know."

"And what—you'll threaten to arrest him?"

"Harassing another person is a crime. I can remind him of that."

She could picture that reminder. Grant could look

pretty fierce when he wanted to. "I'm sure that won't be necessary," she said.

When the bill came, he insisted on paying it, so she left the tip. "It's a nice night," he said. "May I walk you home? I'll walk back for my car."

The request was so formal and old-fashioned. Sweet. "I'd like that," she said.

The streets were mostly empty this time of evening, most of the businesses closed for the day, and traffic was light. They left the main business district and strolled past neat bungalows and cottages, many with broad porches and gingerbread trim, painted in soft pastels. Lights glowed in windows and spilled in golden squares on flower beds blooming with daffodils and crocus. The days were starting to lengthen, though the early evening still held an icy chill. Grant shortened his stride to match hers, a companionable presence.

They stopped on a corner to wait for a light. When the signal changed, she started forward, but he pulled her back. "What's wrong?" she asked, startled.

"Across the street. Do you see him? Look out of the corner of your eye. Pretend to be looking at me."

She turned toward him, looking past him to where a man stood on the opposite corner, watching them. "Is that Toby Masterson?" she asked.

"He's been following us for a couple of blocks, staying back and in the shadows. I wasn't sure at first, but now I am."

"He lives in town. Maybe he's just out for a walk or…" Even as she said the words, she knew they weren't true. Something in Masterson's stance made a shiver run down her spine.

"Wait here," Grant said. "I'll be right back."

Before she could protest, he jogged across the street, against the light. Masterson turned away and tried to flee, but Grant caught up to him easily and grabbed his arm. Masterson resisted, but Grant held firm.

Eve waited until the light changed and crossed the street to join the two men. "What is going on?" she shouted over their raised voices.

"I told him to stop following you," Grant said.

"I just wanted a chance to talk to you," Masterson said. "To warn you again about Dane Trask. He's really dangerous."

Grant started to speak, but Eve sent him a quelling look. "Do you know where Dane is?" she asked. "Have you seen him in town? Have you seen him anywhere near me?"

"That's one of the things I want to talk to you about," Masterson said. "I haven't seen him, but I figure you have. He's probably been trying to get in touch with you."

"Why would Dane get in touch with me?"

"Because he hates you."

The words made her shiver again, but she couldn't believe him. "I haven't seen Dane," she said. "And he hasn't been in touch with me." No need to mention the press release and the deposit box key. That had been so cryptic it hadn't even seemed as if he was communicating with her. She was just a conduit for information he wanted to get out there.

"If he gets in touch with you, you need to let me know," Masterson said. "I can protect you."

"The police will protect her," Grant said.

"Right," Masterson sneered. He turned back to Eve. "Call the hotline number." He shoved a business card at her. "I'm in charge of that program and I'll see you get the protection you need."

"You need to leave now or I'll have you charged with harassment," Grant said.

"And I'll charge you with assault." But Masterson took a step back. "Watch your back, Eve," he said. "You think you know Dane, but you really don't."

He turned and jogged down the sidewalk away from them, disappearing into the dusk.

She stared at the card in her hand, numb. Grant put his arm around her. "Are you okay?" he asked.

"I'm fine." She shoved the card into her coat pocket. "That was just so…strange. Why would he be so certain Dane would want to get in touch with me? If he does, he has my personal and work numbers. He knows where I live. But all I've had is that envelope mailed to the flower shop. Dane might not even have sent it."

"His fingerprints were on the envelope and the press release," Grant said. "We checked."

She shivered, and his grip around her tightened. Comforting, not confining. "Let's get you home," he said.

He kept his arm around her all the way to her house. Once there, he waited while she unlocked the door. "I want to go inside and check around," he said. "Just to reassure us both."

"All right." She stepped back and let him precede her into the front room. He moved through the rooms quickly but deliberately, not commenting on anything he saw, though she had the sense he took in everything. "Does everything look all right to you?" he asked.

"Yes. And you're scaring me a little." She hugged her arms across her chest. "Why should there be anything wrong?"

"I'm just being overly cautious." He returned to where she stood beside the front door and took her by the shoulders. "Being in law enforcement makes you reluctant to trust people's motives," he said. "It's a hazard of the job."

"Are you saying you don't trust me?"

"I don't trust Toby Masterson, and I don't trust Dane Trask. You—I trust you." His gaze searched her face, lingering on her lips.

She leaned into him, drawn by heat and masculinity and her own desire to be closer. To know more. When he dipped his head toward hers she rose up on tiptoe to meet him, her lips pressed to his. He slid his hand from her shoulders around to her back, and pulled her to him. The heat of contact seemed to melt into her, dissolving a stiffness she hadn't even known she'd been holding.

The gentleness of his kiss surprised and touched her, yet when she pressed for more, he responded with a skill and passion that made her sigh. Sensation danced from her lips through the rest of her, until the tips of her fingers tingled and her toes no longer felt the ground. He tasted of wine and spices, and smelled of a subtle aftershave and a fragrance all his own, warm and male and undeniably attractive. She dug her fingers into his shoulders, feeling muscle, and surrendered to the joy of the moment. How long had she been waiting for this and hadn't even realized?

He was the first to pull away, keeping hold of her but putting a little distance between them. "Are you sure you'll be okay alone?" he asked.

Was he hinting that he'd like to stay? As nice as that kiss had been, she wasn't ready for that yet. "I'll be fine," she said. "And thank you for everything."

"Thank you."

He bent his head again, but this time only brushed his lips to her cheek. Then he let himself out. She leaned against the closed door, smiling to herself when she thought she heard him whistle. Grant Sanderlin might be all wrong for her in the long run, but in this moment, he felt very right.

Chapter Eight

"Something's very wrong with this picture," Grant said. He studied the map of the Ranger Brigade's territory, colored pins tracking locations where Dane Trask had supposedly been sighted. At least a dozen pins studded the map, scattered as much as a hundred miles apart.

"These are just the reports we thought were the most reliable," Officer Hudson said. "We set aside all the obvious outliers, like the woman who said she saw an old man with a dog hitchhiking along the highway just outside the entrance to Curecanti Recreation Area. Or the guy who was sure he saw a man disguised as a woman in a café near the lake."

"It doesn't seem likely that one man, traveling on foot, would have covered so much territory in the month he's been missing," Lieutenant Dance said.

"Lotte and I tried tracking around some of the sightings," Rand Knightbridge said, one hand on the head of his search and rescue dog. Lotte, a Belgian

Malinois with black-tipped blond fur and brown eyes that looked as if they had been outlined in kohl, studied the map as intently as any of the human officers. "We didn't find anything. Every trail went cold."

"I put pressure on TDC to share any information they received from their reward hotline," Officer Beck said. "They promised their full cooperation, but then they only turned over a handful of useless reports."

"Maybe that's all they've gotten," Dance said.

"Or maybe they're hoping to find Trask before we do," Beck said. "They strike me as very anxious to have him contained."

"Do you think he has some dirt on them?" Knightbridge asked.

"Don't you?" Beck asked.

"Unless you believe knowing Trask's motives for leaving will help us find him, let's focus this discussion more productively," Grant said. He picked up a pointer and indicated a spot on the national park's southeastern section. "The largest concentration of sightings is in this area," he said.

"It's one of the accessible areas of the park to the public," Dance said. "More people are going to equal more sightings or supposed sightings."

"Why would Trask stay in such a populated area?" Hud asked. "He's a former army ranger. Why not stay in the back country, and reduce the risk of discovery?"

"For a while someone—we assume Trask—was taking food from campers and leaving behind items as a form of payment," Beck said. "The items left have been identified as belonging to Trask."

"The last of those reports occurred ten days ago," Beck said. "Has Trask moved on?"

"He strikes me as too smart to leave any traces behind unless he wants us to see them," Hud said.

"I agree," Grant said. Previously, Trask had left behind items that seemed to be deliberate messages for law enforcement, though Grant wasn't sure they had interpreted all these communications correctly.

"We'll concentrate today's aerial search here." Grant drew a circle an approximate fifty-mile radius from where Trask's truck had crashed in the bottom of the Black Canyon of the Gunnison. "It's unlikely Trask was in that truck when it was driven or pushed into the canyon, so we'll focus our search above the canyon rim. We'll stay away from the campgrounds for now."

"The campground area has the most pins," Hud said.

"We'll be using FLIR to look for a heat signature of a human being," Dance said. The Forward Looking Infrared goggles could be used day or night, and would allow them to see a man who wasn't visible with the naked eye. "If we try that in the campground area, we'll just spot every camper and their dog."

"Trask might come into the campground for

food," Grant said. "But I'm betting he's got a base set up somewhere close by but off the beaten path."

"If he's in a cave, you won't spot him," Knight-bridge said.

"We may not spot him anyway," Grant said. "He could be anywhere out here, or he might have left the country. We just don't know. But we have to start somewhere."

He turned away from the map. "Dance is with me. Beck and Knightbridge, I want you to check out the complaint we got from the Forest Service about traffic through the State Wildlife Area. A car theft ring was using that area last year as a place to stash vehicles until they could part them out or ship them to Mexico. I want to make sure they aren't back in business. Hud, I want you to talk to Audra Trask. See if she's heard anything from her dad, or remembered anything that might help us locate him. Reynolds, are you still working on that antiquities act violation?"

"Yes, sir. I've traced the stolen items to a buyer in Dallas. I have a phone conference set up with him and an agent in Texas this morning." Theft of Native American and ancient peoples' artifacts was an ongoing problem in part of their territory, Grant had learned.

"Good." He checked the duty board. "Redhorse is off today and Reynolds is participating in Rigging for Rescue training over in Ouray. Spencer, you'll need to hold down the fort here."

"Yes, sir."

He could have sent Spencer or anyone else on this surveillance mission. A stack of paperwork several inches thick required his attention and there were those who would have said doing the legwork on a case wasn't the best use of his time. But he had taken a personal interest in this case, and he had never been one to spend all his time sitting behind his desk.

Or maybe it was only that he had a personal interest in Eve Shea. Finding Trask would set her mind at ease and maybe give the two of them a chance to move forward. Anything he could do to make that happen was time well spent in his book.

"You do realize that's the third time you've watered that ivy, don't you?"

Eve blinked at the puddle of water collecting at her feet. How long had she been standing here, drowning the poor plant? Embarrassed, she set aside the watering can and looked around for something to wipe up the spill.

"I've got it," Sarah said, and began tearing off paper towels and using them to blot the spill. "Everything okay with you?"

"I'm fine," Eve said, though in truth she was groggy from a lack of sleep. Her evening with Grant—and the kiss that had ended the night—had left her tossing and turning. If only he were younger. If only he wasn't already a father. If only, if only…

When she had finally fallen asleep, she had been disturbed by dreams featuring the Ranger Brigade commander and Dane, facing off with swords in an arena full of spectators. By the time her alarm had gone off this morning, she had been anything but refreshed.

Sarah finished mopping up the water and stood. "Okay, I was going to keep quiet and not be my usual nosy self, but now I have to know. What happened on your date last night?"

It was a question she and Sarah had discussed dozens of times in the last six months. Eve had welcomed the chance to rehash and analyze her many dates.

But last night felt different. "It wasn't a date," she said. "He wanted to fill me in on some developments in the case."

"Sure he did." Sarah's smile produced deep dimples at the corners of her mouth. "That's why he showered and shaved and got dressed up to come see you in person instead of making a phone call."

Eve didn't try to argue. "We had a nice dinner at the Sherpa," she said.

Sarah nodded. "Okay. Not fancy, but good. Did you enjoy it?"

"It was all right." She stowed the watering can under the front counter and took out a roll of ribbon and scissors. With prom season just around the corner, it wouldn't hurt to get a head start on making corsage bows.

"Did he kiss you?"

The scissors slipped and she narrowly missed nicking her wrist. She'd sliced the ribbon crookedly, and focused on evening it up. "That's none of your business."

"Which must mean yes." Sarah didn't sound offended. "And since you have never balked at sharing details with me before, I think this man must be someone special."

"I hardly know him," Eve protested.

"The heart knows before the mind does, sometimes."

"Is that supposed to be profound?" Eve asked. "Because it doesn't even make sense."

Sarah smiled and disappeared into the back room. Eve glared after her. As much as she loved her friend, the woman could be insufferable.

The front door chimed and Cara Mead, dressed in a paisley wrap dress and chunky sandals, strolled in. "Cara, it's good to see you," Eve said, grateful as much for a reprieve from Sarah's questions as she was to see her friend. "Did you come to talk about flowers for your wedding?" Yesterday, Cara had asked if Eve could provide the flowers for her wedding to Ranger Brigade officer Jason Beck in the fall.

"I don't really have time today," Cara said. "But we should definitely make time soon. I'm hoping you'll have some ideas, because I'm drawing a blank."

"It helps to consider the season and your budget. And you might try keeping a notebook where you jot down ideas of things you've seen or read about, and you want to copy for your wedding."

Cara nodded. "I'll ask Jason what he thinks, too."

"Good idea." Some grooms wanted to be more involved in weddings these days. "If you didn't come to talk flowers, what else can I do for you?"

"I wanted to thank you for participating in our protest yesterday," Cara said. "It really helped with our numbers. It looked good on TV, and the higher-ups like that."

"I was glad to help," Eve said.

"I'm hoping I can persuade you to do another favor for me," Cara said, coming to stand across the front counter from Eve.

"Do you need a donation for a fundraiser?" Eve asked. "I could do that."

"That's very generous of you, but no," Cara said. "I need a volunteer. Someone to go up to the mine with me to collect soil, water and rock samples for testing."

"Is that legal?" Cara asked. "Isn't that private property?"

"I own stock in TDC," Cara said. "It was part of my compensation package. While the mine is private property, TDC is in charge of it while they're doing mitigation. As a TDC stockholder, I think I have a right to check their work."

"I'm not sure TDC would agree," Eve said.

"Probably not." She shrugged.

"What does Jason say?"

"I haven't told him I plan to collect more samples," she said. "I'm not sure he'd understand."

"I don't know," Eve said.

"Please!" Cara leaned closer, her voice lower. "I can't ask just anyone. It has to be someone I trust. And I really think this is important."

"Of course protecting the environment is important, but—"

"I don't mean for the environment," Cara said. "I mean for Dane. I think he discovered something at the Mary Lee that wasn't right, but when he tried to reveal his findings, his life was threatened and he had to go into hiding. If we can figure out what he found and go public with the information, Dane can come home."

Eve stared at the younger woman. The whole proposal sounded like some wild fantasy. "Dane wasn't the type to run from danger," she said. Then again, he had never struck her as the type to be vague or play silly games. Which made his recent behavior all the more baffling.

"Dane is smart," Cara said. "And resourceful. He's doing what he believes he has to do."

Then I wish he'd leave me out of it, Eve thought. But Cara had sparked her curiosity. "If I agree to help you, what do I have to do?" she asked.

"Go on a hike with me. I know a back way into

the mine site. We'll slip in, collect the samples and be gone in a matter of minutes."

"Dane should have never involved either of us in this," Eve said. "I wish he hadn't."

"But he did," Cara said. "I think it's because he knew we would help him." She smiled. "Help me out and when he comes back home we'll both chew him out about it."

"Why are you so set on doing this?" Eve asked. "Do you think you'll get your old job back when Dane returns? Do you even want that?"

"I just…" Cara shook her head, then took a deep breath and said, "My brother was murdered in Houston—years ago. His murderer was never found, and as bad as losing him was, knowing I couldn't do anything to help him was worse. Now Dane is accused of all these things I don't believe he did. If there's something I can do to help him, I'm not going to pass up the chance."

"I'm sorry about your brother," Eve said. "But I can't help you." She would have done a lot for her former lover, but this was too much. And when she saw Dane again—and she had to believe she would—she would tell him so. Maybe they'd have a laugh about it.

Or maybe he would tell her she had let him down. It was a risk she was willing to take.

GRANT AND DANCE met the helicopter pilot at a crop-spraying outfit on the edge of town. When he wasn't

spraying farmers' fields, the pilot subcontracted for
the government for search and rescue, fire-spotting,
and searches like this one.

"You've got a good clear day for this," the pilot
said as they readied for takeoff.

Grant said nothing, merely kept his focus straight
ahead, intent on breathing evenly. He had never enjoyed flying, and the sensation of hovering over the
earth in what he couldn't help think of as a giant mechanical mosquito did nothing to ease his discomfort.

They soared out over rock canyons and alkaline
washes, crossing into a landscape of pale green prai-
rie dotted with clumps of dark green trees. Then
suddenly, a dark gash split the earth below. The helicopter swung wide and they were over the canyon, a
dark shape like a salamander winding beneath them,
its legs side canyons, the thin sliver of the Gunnison
River far below a silver stripe down its back.

"That's a sight I never get tired of," the pilot said
in Grant's headset. "We're almost at your coordi-
nates."

"I've got the FLIR ready," Dance said. "Do you
want to take a look?"

Grant took the goggles and fit them on, and studied the images below. Swirls of colors swam in his
vision, before taking shape like the patterns on a
weather map. Dots of red scattered as the helicopter
flew over—a herd of deer or antelope. He focused

on another red dot, moving much slower along a dull yellow strip.

"Bicyclist, along the park road," Dance said, scanning with a pair of high-powered binoculars.

"Trask won't be along the road," Grant said. "Move out."

The helicopter turned, chased by its own shadow across more barren terrain now. For ten minutes they flew in a broad arc, but the goggles—and Dance's binoculars—registered no sign of life.

"Wait a minute, I've got something," Dance said from his position behind the pilot. "Not a person, but something that shouldn't be there. Can you bring us in a little lower?"

"Will do."

Grant's stomach lurched into his throat as the helicopter dropped. He pulled off the goggles and looked past the pilot as the aircraft tilted, giving him a view of what looked like a garbage dump.

"What is that?" Grant asked.

"Illegal dump site." Dance lowered the binoculars, scowling. "Looks like construction waste. You can see the track the trucks hauling it have cut across the ground." He indicated a route Grant had mistaken for a forest service road.

"Is that in the national park?" the pilot asked.

"It's in the recreation area," Dance said. "It wasn't there the last time I was in this sector."

"When was that?" Grant asked.

"Two and a half, maybe three months ago."

"Want to take another look?" the pilot asked.

"Michael?" Grant asked Dance.

"I've got a good idea of where it's located," Dance said. "We'll get more information on the ground."

"Take us back to base," Grant said. "I don't think the man we're looking for is here." They would need a tremendous amount of luck to find someone who didn't want to be found in this massive territory, but he had felt a flyover was worth a shot. Maybe Trask had seen them and realized they weren't going to give up looking for him.

Back at Ranger Brigade headquarters, Lieutenant Dance began organizing a team to collect evidence from the illegal dump site. "If we're lucky, who-ever did this left something behind that will help us identify them. At the very least, we should be able to determine if this is an active site that they're still adding to. If that's the case, we can set up a stake-out to catch them."

Grant returned to his office to tackle some of the paperwork that was the inevitable burden of com-mand. He had just opened a new file on his computer when his phone buzzed. "Commander Sanderlin."

"Pete McCabe, with the National Park," a deep voice said. "We've got a situation over here we need to pull you in on."

Grant sat up straighter. "What's the situation?"

"We've got a DB found on one of the trails. A woman, late twenties. Her throat's been cut."

"I'll send someone right over."

"Just so you know, I think this might relate to something you're already working on."

"How's that?"

"We found a business card clutched in the woman's hand. A card for Dane Trask."

Chapter Nine

Grant looked down on the body of the young woman at the side of the trail. Arms flung back, lifeless eyes staring vacantly to the sky, it was hard to picture the beautiful, vibrant person she might have been. "The cut was made with a large-bladed knife, like a hunting knife." The medical examiner, a middle-aged woman with short blond hair, spoke matter-of-factly as she stripped off blue nitrile gloves. "No signs of trouble that I can see. Not even any scuff marks in the dirt. I think he surprised her from behind. She was probably dead before she had time to register what was happening."

Grant pictured it: the woman hiking along, admiring the scenery around her, the man seizing her, perhaps lifting her off her feet, slicing open her throat, then laying her out here beside the trail, as if on display. She lay in the shade, on a bed of pinion needles, their forest-fresh smell wafting up to mingle with the stench of death.

He turned to the park ranger beside him. McCabe was in his late fifties, his tanned face creased with fine lines, his hazel eyes almost lost in the many folds. "You said there was a business card?"

"Here." McCabe passed over a clear evidence bag. The card inside was white, with a red-and-black logo for Welcome Home Warriors and the name Dane Trask, with a phone number, in black lettering underneath.

"Looks like Trask left this deliberately," McCabe said. "I don't know if he's taunting us or what."

Grant slipped the evidence bag with the card into his jacket and looked at the woman again. "Who is she?"

"Marsha Grandberry, aged twenty-two, a student at Western State, according to the ID in the wallet she had with her."

"Did she know Dane Trask?" Grant asked.

McCabe shrugged. "That's for you to find out."

Jason Beck, who had been talking to a small group of civilians gathered behind the barriers the park service had set up at the trailhead two miles back, came loping down the trail. "What have you got?" Grant asked.

"Her boyfriend and her best friend—her roommate, actually—are back there waiting," he said. "They came as soon as they got the word from one of the rangers. They both say Marsha didn't know Trask. She didn't have any connection to Welcome

Home Warriors or to TDC Enterprises. She was studying botany and came here today to get some photos she needed for a presentation she was working on for a class." He had been avoiding looking at the body, but glanced that way now as two technicians lifted the shrouded figure onto a gurney. "Why would Trask kill her like that?"

"We don't know that the murderer was Trask," Grant said.

Beck nodded. "He must have handed out a lot of business cards. So you think someone is trying to make him look guilty?"

"This is an area of the park where we've had the most sightings of Trask," McCabe said. "And the knife sounds like something a former army ranger would have."

"Anyone who's been following this case knows those things," Grant said. "But we also know that Trask is smart. He hasn't done anything I've seen so far without a reason."

"Like I told you, he left the card to taunt us," McCabe said. "He thinks he's smarter than law enforcement."

"He didn't have a reason to kill Marsha Grandberry," Beck said. "No one I've interviewed about him has mentioned anything about violence."

Toby Masterson had warned Eve that Trask was violent, but his accusations hadn't rung true to Grant. Still, he couldn't discard them. "We'll check the card for fingerprints and the body and the surroundings for any DNA or other evidence," he said. "We're not ruling out any suspect at this point."

He left Beck to oversee the forensics team and headed back down the trail to his waiting cruiser. Sun beat down on the back of his neck, and his boots crunched in the red gravel of the trail. If Trask had murdered this woman, a stranger to him, then he was indeed as dangerous as Masterson had warned. Was he a danger to Eve as well?

Grant needed to call and break this news to her before she read about it in the paper, and reiterate his warning for her to be careful.

Head down, preoccupied with these thoughts, he was startled to hear a woman's voice call his name.

"Grant!"

He jerked his head up as Eve jogged toward him. Her face was drawn with worry. "A colleague at the paper called to tell me he'd just heard the rangers found a woman murdered in the park." She gripped his arm, fingers digging into his muscle through the thick fabric of his jacket. "He said they think Dane killed her. That has to be wrong. He wouldn't do something like that."

Aware of people looking in their direction, some of them probably from the media, Grant put one hand at her back and steered her around to the passenger side of his cruiser. "Let's go to headquarters where we can talk privately," he said. "I'll bring you back to your car later." She didn't look in a fit state to drive right now. She slid into the passenger seat and buckled the safety belt, lips pressed tightly together, as if she was struggling to hold back a flood of words. That was one of the things he appreciated about Eve: she knew how to be patient, how to wait for the right time to speak, and she hadn't shown a tendency to jump to conclusions.

Indeed, she waited until they were in his office with the door closed before she spoke. "Dane wouldn't kill someone," she said. "Not unless it was in self-defense. Was this self-defense?"

Grant sat, not in the chair behind his desk, but in a side chair. He motioned for her to take the chair beside him. "This wasn't in self-defense," he said. "And don't ask for more details, because I can't tell you."

She visibly shuddered. "I don't want details. But do you really think Dane killed her? Why?"

He spoke slowly, choosing his words carefully. It was always a balance, giving those close to a case the information they wanted, and protecting evidence in a criminal case. "There was something left at the scene that might have belonged to Dane," he said. "It's one piece of what will eventually be a whole body of evidence. It doesn't mean Dane is guilty."

"But it doesn't mean he's innocent, either," she said. "And you don't have to speak so circumspectly. My reporter friend told me one of Dane's business cards was left on the body."

"How did he know that? Who is this reporter?" Anger tinged Grant's words.

"I'll give you his name, but don't be angry with him. He said an anonymous caller phoned the paper. He called the park and they confirmed they had found a dead woman, but wouldn't say more."

"What's his name?" Grant grabbed a pen and a pad of paper from the corner of his desk.

She gave him the name and phone number of her friend. "Do you think you can trace the call?" she asked.

"Probably not," he admitted. They would try, but a brief call, probably made from a cell phone, was unlikely to yield much information. "But we'll want to know exactly what was said, what the call sounded like, and things like that." So much of investigating a crime was collecting as much information as possible, never knowing which piece might be the one to complete the puzzle.

"Dane wouldn't kill someone," she said again. "And he certainly wouldn't call a reporter and brag about it. I was always after him to do more to promote Welcome Home Warriors in the media. The only time he ever sent out a press release about the group was when I wrote it for him. He really isn't someone who seeks the limelight."

"If I had asked you before all this happened, you would have said he wouldn't purposely wreck his truck, abandon his home and daughter to live in the wilderness, raiding campsites for food and sending cryptic messages about his former employer," Grant said.

"He isn't raiding campsites," she said. "Cara told me he always leaves something of value, which I think shows what an honest and honorable man he is."

Hearing her defend her former lover abraded Grant's nerves like sandpaper. "You didn't answer my question," he said. "You have to admit what Dane Trask has done is not normal behavior."

She bowed her head, hands clasped tightly in her lap. "No," she said softly. "It isn't. But that doesn't make him a murderer."

"We're going to do everything we can to find the person who did this," Grant said. "The right person."

She nodded, and sniffed. His chest tightened. Was she going to cry? Because of something he'd said?

But when she lifted her head, her eyes were dry. "Is there anything I can do to help?" she asked.

He hesitated, then slipped the evidence bag from his pocket and showed it to her. "Do you recognize this?" he asked.

She stared at the card, swallowed hard, then nodded. "Dane carried those with him everywhere." Her eyes met his. "He must have handed out hundreds of them. He gave them to every veteran he met, to families and friends of veterans, to potential employers, to donors. He even pinned them on bulletin boards and left them with tips at restaurants. He tried hard to directly reach people he could help, even though he resisted dealing with the media." She looked at the card again. "Anyone could have put that card there to throw suspicion on Dane. But if he did kill that woman, he wouldn't leave his card. That's just stupid."

"Maybe he wanted us to know. Maybe he was taunting us, letting us know we'd never catch him."

"He wasn't like that." She sounded exhausted, her shoulders slumped. "I know you haven't seen evidence of that, but Dane was a really good man."

"If he was so good, why did you break up with him?"

He hadn't meant to speak the words out loud. Eve stared at him. "I told you why Dane and I split up. But maybe you don't believe me. Maybe you don't want to believe me." She stood.

He reached out, as if to stop her, but the look in her eyes froze him. "I'm sorry," he said. "I shouldn't have said that."

She turned away. "I'd better go now."

He stood also. "I'll take you back to your car."

"I'll ask one of your officers to do it. I'm sure you have more important work to do."

"I'll call you tonight," he said.

"Don't." She shook her head. "It would really be better if you didn't."

She walked out of the office, shutting the door firmly behind her. He stared after her, fury warring with shame. The one woman he'd met in forever he felt a true connection with, and he'd let stupid jealousy—

over a man she was no longer with—ruin things. Was he forty-five or fourteen? He ran his fingers through his hair and dropped into the chair behind his desk. When he found Dane Trask, he was going to punch him. Or maybe Trask should punch him. It was a toss-up which would feel more deserved.

TWO DAYS LATER, Eve stared at the headline on the front page of the local newspaper. HUNT FOR TRASK INTENSIFIES AS WOMAN FOUND MURDERED IN NATIONAL PARK. The story below the headline named Dane as the chief suspect in the death of Marsha Grandberry, a local college student. Eve felt sick as she read the details of the crime, and had to sit down.

For once she was alone in the shop, Sarah having taken the morning off for a dentist appointment. Of course her friend would ask questions about this latest development, but at least Eve would have time to absorb this new information and come up with some kind of response. But what could she possibly say? She and Dane were no longer close. She had no idea what was going through his mind these days. Was it possible he had snapped and was indeed responsible for a woman's death?

The bell connected to the front door sounded and she looked up, smile pasted on her face, prepared to greet a customer and pretend nothing out of the ordinary had happened. The smile dropped when she recognized Cara Mead. "You've seen the paper," Cara said, nodding at the sheets open on the counter in front of Eve.

"Yes, and I can't believe it," Eve said.

"You can't believe it because it isn't true," Cara said. "Dane wouldn't kill anyone, much less a woman he didn't know who wasn't hurting anyone." She slid onto the high stool at the front counter and dropped her purse to the floor beside her. "And all that nonsense about one of Dane's business cards being left behind. As if he's a complete idiot, or a homicidal maniac."

"I don't know what to think," Eve said.

"*I* think someone is trying to frame him," Cara said. "Someone else killed that woman, in an area where Dane had been spotted, and left his business card—which anyone might have because we both know Dane handed out hundreds of the things— so that the police would think Dane was the killer."

"But why do that?" Eve asked.

"So the police would look harder for him? So that if they caught him they would be less likely to listen to anything he had to say." She leaned across the counter and spoke with a new urgency. "That's why we have to go back up to the Mary Lee Mine and get those samples. All the clues Dane has sent us point to something not right—maybe even downright criminal—going on up there. He's counting on us to prove him right."

"So he's letting us do his dirty work?" The bitterness in her voice startled Eve. She had thought she was over being angry or annoyed with Dane and his tendency to be so focused on what he wanted, and what he thought was right, even if others didn't agree. He wanted to go to Mexico on vacation and listed ten reasons why her desire to go to Hawaii instead was a bad idea. He didn't like seafood so they never went to seafood restaurants, even if there were other things on the menu he could have ordered. He had decided he didn't want children and her opinion didn't matter.

"He must have a good reason," Cara said. "Dane was never a coward."

True. Though he had his faults, Dane never backed down from a challenge. If he was wrong, he admitted it and apologized. And he had fought for his country, in some very dangerous places.

But that didn't mean she had to put herself in danger. "I'm sorry, but I don't think more samples are going to prove anything," she said. "We'd better leave this to the Ranger Brigade and local police."

Cara looked disappointed, but not particularly surprised. "Let me know if you change your mind," she said. "I can't just sit around and do nothing. I have to try to help."

"Good luck," Eve said. "But maybe, since Dane got himself into this mess—whatever it is—he's the only one who can get himself out."

Chapter Ten

Grant surveyed the mounds of rubble scattered over half an acre of what had been, until recently, pristine wilderness. Broken concrete, old timbers, tons of rock ranging from fist-sized chunks to man-sized boulders, were scattered amid the stunted pinions and red rock formations. Deep ruts cut through the sagebrush showed the path of the trucks that had dumped the debris here. The sun beat down on it all, spring fast turning to summer here in the high desert.

"This has all been left here in the last month, I'm sure," Lieutenant Dance said. He nudged an irregular chunk of gray rock with one foot. "I did a patrol down the only road back in here about a month ago and I'm sure I would have noticed those tracks leading from it back here."

Jason Beck picked up a chunk of yellow-gray rock and examined it. "This looks like the same stuff that was at the Mary Lee Mine," he said.

"Wasn't some of that material radioactive?" Dance asked.

Beck tossed the rock aside. "It was. We ought to have this stuff tested."

"I don't know." Dance looked around. "Wasn't the stuff at the mine just rock? This has wood and metal, and I think there's even some Sheetrock over there." He pointed toward the farthest mound. "This looks more like construction debris than anything from a mine."

"So who would dump construction debris all the way out here?" Grant asked. "It's a long way from town to haul all of this."

"Bids for projects usually include the cost of disposal," Dance said. "Landfills charge by the yard and for a big project that can really add up. Dump the stuff out here and you pocket the extra." He scowled. "And the chances of anyone catching you in the act are slim to none."

"Unfortunately, this kind of thing happens on public land all the time," Beck said. "Mostly it's just a bag of household trash or a broken appliance. People don't want to deal with it, so they dump it somewhere out of the way and make it someone else's problem."

"It doesn't usually happen on this scale," Dance said. "This goes way beyond a little littering."

"Maybe if we test it, we can determine where it came from," Beck said.

"We can't test every rock," Dance argued.

"We'll test a few samples," Grant said. "But we don't have the budget to test everything. I think our best bet is to get officers to watch the area for a few days and nights, patrol the area more frequently, maybe see if we can get a camera or two out here and see if we can come up with anything."

"They might be done dumping," Dance said.

"They might, but if they've gotten away with this so far, they might decide to continue," Grant said. "They might believe they've found a good way to make some extra money without a lot of hassle."

"If I find them, they'll know hassle," Dance said. "It's going to cost the government—in other words, taxpayers—a fortune to clean all this up."

"We'll hold off on cleanup for a bit," Grant said. "Let's see if the people responsible for this show up."

"I'll make a schedule for surveillance and see about setting up a couple of cameras," Dance said.

"I can find out who's got a big construction project going on in the area," Beck said. "This isn't a simple house build, unless it's a monster of a house."

"Good thinking," Grant said. He left Beck and Dance to hash out details while he returned to his cruiser. But he didn't leave right away. He pulled out some paperwork to complete, but sat with it resting beside him, as he stared out at the landscape of turreted stone and sage-covered hills. So different from any view he ever had in DC.

But then, he had wanted a change. A fresh start.

His thoughts turned to Eve. She could have no doubt how he felt about her after the kiss they had shared, but still she held back. He thought he knew why—despite her protests, she was still in love with Dane Trask. Even after his disappearing act, the manipulative SOB had his hold on her, getting her entangled in his troubles.

His radio crackled. "Commander?" Dance's voice emerged from the static.

"I hear you," Grant answered.

"Hang on a minute. I've got something you should see."

Grant looked up and thought he could make out a figure in the distance moving toward him. After a moment, he could recognize Dance, carrying something in one hand.

Grant stepped out of the cruiser to meet his officer. "We just found this up under some of the construction debris," Dance said. He held out a clear evidence pouch. In it was a torn, muddy piece of eight-and-a-half-by-eleven paper with a crude crayon drawing. Grant studied the figure in the drawing, which might have been a man or a monster or even a robot—red crayon tracing a boxy, broad-shouldered figure with an oversize head and a wild tangle of black hair. "It looks like a kid's drawing," he said, returning it to Dance.

"I don't think it came from a mine," Dance said.

"There's a name on it." He pointed to a scribble in the corner that Grant hadn't picked up on. "Max" was scrawled in a pale green crayon.

"Log it in," Grant said. "Maybe we can connect it to someone." He opened the cruiser door. "Let me know if you find anything else like this."

"Yes, sir."

Dance went back to the search and Grant started the cruiser's engine. That kid's drawing had made the hairs on the back of his neck stand up. It was so out of place out here. He tried to shake off the feeling. That was the thing about this job. Do it long enough and pretty soon it was easy to see even something innocent as sinister.

EVE LOOKED UP from an anniversary arrangement she was finishing to greet the customer who had just walked in. She was surprised, and pleased, to see Audra Trask. Audra, Dane's twenty-three-year-old daughter, had her father's blue eyes, dark hair and delicate features that must have come from her mother. Audra had always been friendly and welcoming to Eve, never the stereotype of the jealous only child. "It's so wonderful to see you," Eve said, coming out from behind the counter to embrace the younger woman.

"I've been meaning to stop by and say hello for months now and time keeps getting away from me," Audra said.

"I'm glad you finally made it," Eve said. "What have you been up to?"

"I've been super busy with the preschool." Audra ran a hand through her hair, though this did nothing to tame her thick mane. "That's why I'm here, actually. I need to order some flowers for our parents' luncheon on the twenty-first."

"I'm sure I can help you." Eve moved behind the counter once more and took out an order form. "Do you have something particular in mind?"

"No. I'm hoping you can help me decide."

"Tell me your budget and how many arrangements you're looking for and we'll see what we can come up with."

For the next half hour they looked through photographs of possible arrangements and discussed the merits of carnations versus daisies, possible color combinations and possible vases. Audra settled on six table arrangements in ceramic containers that resembled stacks of alphabet blocks, with yellow daisies, blue delphinium and white carnations. "Those are going to be perfect," Audra declared as she signed the order forms. "And at the end of the luncheon, I'll give away the arrangements as door prizes. That way I won't have to worry about storing and moving those cute vases."

"You're moving?" Eve asked. She separated the multipart form and slid Audra's copy across to her.

"Only down the street. I'm going to have a brand-new facility, as part of the new elementary school."

"That's wonderful. When will you be moving?"

"We're supposed to be in the new place by the end of August." She folded the papers and slipped them into her purse. "I can't wait. Business has been good, so we could use the extra space. Hey, you should stop by some time and I'll give you a tour of the new place."

"I'd love that."

She expected Audra to say goodbye and leave, but the young woman lingered. "I guess you've heard all this stuff in the news about Dad," she said.

"Yes." Eve kept her expression guarded. "It's been a real shock."

"It's been horrible!" Audra hugged her arms across her middle. "I don't know why Dad disappeared, but whatever is going on, he's not a murderer. You know he isn't."

"I know," Eve agreed. No matter what scenario she put together in her mind, she could never come up with one in which Dane would cut the throat of a woman—especially one she was sure he didn't know.

"And all these stories I keep reading about Dad hiding out in the wilderness, stealing campers' food and stuff." Audra shook her head. "It's ridiculous. If Dad did run away, for whatever reason, why wouldn't he skip to the Caribbean or South America or something? Sure, he always liked hiking and camping, but nobody likes it that much."

Audra's indignation almost made Eve smile. "Have you heard from your father at all?" she asked.

"Not a word. Which kind of ticks me off when I think about it, you know? I mean, he slipped his admin, Cara, a couple of flash drives but he couldn't even drop me—his daughter—a note to let me know he's okay." She studied Eve. "Have you heard from him?"

"It wasn't like a personal note or anything," Eve said. "He sent me a press release accusing TDC of cutting corners with their mine mitigation project. I think he sent it to me because I used to work for the paper."

"Huh." Audra frowned. "This whole thing is just crazy. I'm worried about him and scared for him and I really don't have time for any of it."

"Exactly," Eve said. "I couldn't have said it better."

Audra flashed a brief smile. "Good. When he gets back, we can take turns yelling at him." She hitched her purse up higher on her shoulder. "I'd better get going. It was good to see you again."

"It was good to see you, too."

Audra left and Eve returned to work on the anniversary arrangement. When the doorbell sounded again, she expected it to be her customer, picking up his order, but when she looked up, she was startled to see Toby Masterson, all charismatic smile and rugged good looks.

"Hello, Eve," he said. He crossed to the front counter and rested both palms on the top. Heart pounding, she leaned away from him, determined not the show fear. "I think it's past time you and I had a little talk."

"I have nothing to say to you, Mr. Masterson." Eve said. She focused on the flower arrangement, doing her best to ignore him.

"Actually, I came in to buy some flowers," Masterson said.

Eve wasn't sure she believed him, but she would play along. "What can I get for you?" she asked.

"What do you think is appropriate for an apology?" he asked.

"Roses are a classic," she said. "Though it depends on the recipient and what he or she likes."

"What do you like?" he asked, moving closer, until only the counter separated them.

Eve forced herself to meet Masterson's gaze. "I don't like men who play games," she said. "Or those who lie to me. I especially don't like those who threaten me."

He held up both hands in a gesture of surrender. "Whoa. I never threatened you."

"You said Dane was a threat, which was just as bad."

"I'm sorry if I came on too strong the first couple of times we met." His smile turned ingratiating. "I tend to do that whenever I'm really passionate about a subject."

She didn't return the smile. "Apology accepted. Now I really do have to get back to work." She picked up a spike of lemon grass and pretended to study the arrangement in progress. But she was hyperaware of the man across the counter. She could smell the exotic fragrance of his cologne, mixed with a hint of mint. Chewing gum? A breath mint?

"I'd like to start over with you," he said. "The truth is, beautiful women always make me nervous."

It could have been the worst pickup line ever, but he managed to make it sound sincere. "What do you want, Mr. Masterson?" she asked.

"Toby," he said. "And really, all I want is to go out with you."

She stared at him. "Do you mean a date?"

"Yeah." He tucked both hands in the front pockets of his jeans and rocked back on his heels. "To tell you the truth, I was always jealous of Dane. I saw him with you a couple of times and stupid as it sounds, I developed this big crush on you." He put a hand over his heart. "I really thought I was too old for that kind of thing, but I guess not." Another smile, endearing this time.

Eve had to admit, he was getting to her. "You saw me with Dane?"

"At Welcome Home Warriors headquarters. You didn't see me. I was just another guy in the background. But you just struck me right away as someone special. And I don't know—I thought he kind of took you for granted." He shrugged. "Maybe that was just wishful thinking on my part."

Dane had taken her for granted. It was one of the things they had argued about, at the end, after he had made it clear no one could change his mind about having more children.

"When I heard the two of you had broken up, I wasted months working up the nerve to ask you out myself," Masterson said. "And then Dane did his disappearing act and I got really worried about you."

"Dane had his faults, but he was never violent," she said. "Certainly not toward me."

"Well, you probably know him better than I did." He took his hands out of his pockets and rested them on the counter once more. "So will you give me another chance? Let me take you to dinner. One date. If it doesn't work out, I promise I'll take it like a man."

For some reason, his choice of words amused her. Still, she was reluctant to say yes.

Masterson's expression sobered. "You're not involved with anyone, are you?" he asked. "That guy you were with the other night?"

The mention of Grant sent a pain through her. She was so attracted to him—and he was so wrong for her.

She remembered what Sarah had said about Eve having a type. Toby Masterson, with his rugged good looks and military background, was cut from the same cloth as Dane. Maybe she could be attracted to him if she let herself. And she had vowed to date anyone who asked her out until she found the man. "All right," she said. "I'll have dinner with you."

He grinned, and took a step back from the counter. "That's terrific. Is tomorrow night okay? I could pick you up at your place, or here."

"My place would be fine."

She gave him her address and he left the shop and almost swaggered down the sidewalk. Dane had walked like that sometimes, a man in command of his world.

She shouldn't think about Dane now, or whatever had gone wrong with his world. She was making a new life now. Maybe Toby Masterson could be a part of it.

MITCH RUFFINO REMINDED Grant of a scrappy terrier— the kind who growled at anyone who came near, and puffed up its hair to make itself as large as possible. While the vice president of TDC Enterprises didn't exactly growl when Grant entered his office, he did scowl, throw back his shoulders, and make it clear he didn't want this meeting to go on any longer than necessary. "Instead of wasting your time questioning me, you should be out there finding Dane Trask," he said. "The man is a thief and a murderer."

The Montrose County Sheriff's Department was investigating the embezzlement charges against Trask, so Grant was unfamiliar with the evidence in the case. The Ranger Brigade's investigation into the murder of Marsha Grandberry was stalled due to a lack of evidence. Whether or not Trask was the murderer, the Rangers were actively trying to find him because he was someone who had gone missing in their jurisdiction. "We are doing everything we can to locate Trask," he said, no contrition or apology in his tone. He was merely stating fact. And his next words, though some might have read them as conciliatory, held the same note of command. "It would be helpful if you would share whatever tips you've gleaned from your reward hotline."

"I doubt we've received anything that would be of use to you," Ruffino said.

"Nevertheless, I want to see what you have."

Ruffino made a motion as if he was shooing away a fly. "Of course. I'll get back to you on that."

Which wasn't exactly a promise to cooperate, but Grant wouldn't press. "Tell me about Dane Trask's work," he said.

Ruffino's nostrils flared, and Grant was reminded again of a dog. "What do you mean?" he asked.

"What exactly did he do? What was he working on before he disappeared? Who was he close to? How did he have access to the funds you're accusing him of embezzling?"

"I don't see that any of that is relevant." Ruffino tapped his fingertips impatiently on the desktop.

Get Up To 4 Free Books!

Dear Reader,

IT'S A FACT: if you answer 4 quick questions, we'll send you 4 FREE REWARDS from each series you try!

Try **Harlequin® Romantic Suspense** books featuring heart-racing page-turners with unexpected plot twists and irresistible chemistry that will keep you guessing to the very end.

Try **Harlequin Intrigue® Larger-Print** books featuring action-packed stories that will keep you on the edge of your seat. Solve the crime and deliver justice at all costs.

Or **TRY BOTH!**

I'm not kidding you. As a leading publisher of women's fiction, we value your opinions... and your time. That's why we are prepared to reward you handsomely for completing our mini-survey. In fact, we have 4 Free Rewards for you, including 2 free books and 2 free gifts from each series you try!

Thank you for participating in our survey,

Pam Powers

To get your 4 FREE REWARDS:
Complete the survey below and return the insert today to receive up to 4 FREE BOOKS and FREE GIFTS guaranteed!

DETACH AND MAIL CARD TODAY!

"4 for 4" MINI-SURVEY

1 Is reading one of your favorite hobbies?
YES ☐ NO ☐

2 Do you prefer to read instead of watch TV?
YES ☐ NO ☐

3 Do you read newspapers and magazines?
YES ☐ NO ☐

4 Do you enjoy trying new book series with FREE BOOKS?
YES ☐ NO ☐

Please send me my Free Rewards, consisting of **2 Free Books from each series I select** and **Free Mystery Gifts**. I understand that I am under no obligation to buy anything, as explained on the back of this card.

- ☐ **Harlequin® Romantic Suspense** (240/340 HDL GQ5A)
- ☐ **Harlequin Intrigue® Larger-Print** (199/399 HDL GQ5A)
- ☐ **Try Both** (240/340 & 199/399 HDL GQ5M)

FIRST NAME

LAST NAME

ADDRESS

APT.#

CITY

STATE/PROV.

ZIP/POSTAL CODE

EMAIL ☐ Please check this box if you would like to receive newsletters and promotional emails from Harlequin Enterprises ULC and its affiliates. You can unsubscribe anytime.

Your Privacy – Your information is being collected by Harlequin Enterprises ULC, operating as Reader Service. For a complete summary of the information we collect, how we use this information and to whom it is disclosed, please visit our privacy notice located at https://corporate.harlequin.com/privacy-notice. From time to time we may also exchange your personal information with reputable third parties. If you wish to opt out of this sharing of your personal information, please visit www.readerservice.com/consumerschoice or call 1-800-873-8635. **Notice to California Residents** – Under California law, you have specific rights to control and access your data. For more information on these rights and how to exercise them, visit https://corporate.harlequin.com/california-privacy.

HI/HRS-520-MS20

HARLEQUIN READER SERVICE—Here's how it works:

"I'm trying to get an idea of his frame of mind, and what might have triggered him to leave."

"You already know that," Ruffino said. "He left because he realized his theft had been discovered and he would soon be arrested. He ran like the coward he is."

"His military record isn't that of a coward," Grant said. Trask had received several commendations and silver and bronze stars during his military career. None of his actions even now struck Grant as those of a coward.

"Civilian life is very different from the military," Ruffino said, though Grant doubted the man had ever served. "But to answer your question, he was working on several projects for us, none of which could have been related to his disappearance. They were very routine. The kind of thing TDC does every day."

"Which projects, specifically?"

"I don't know offhand. I'll have to get back to you on that."

"Given your interest in Trask, I would have thought you would know exactly what he was working on before he left," Grant said.

Ruffino's gaze hardened. "Then you'd be wrong." He snatched a sheaf of papers from his in-box and tapped them pointedly on the desktop. "I'm a very busy man and I really can't help you. If I knew anything that could aid in finding Trask, he would be found—and in prison, where he belongs."

"Acting uncooperative is a good way to hide what

you do know," Grant said. "But it's not a technique that works for very long." He took a step back, toward the door, but keeping his gaze fixed on Ruffino. "Whatever it is you don't want me to know, I'm going to find out. And I'm going to remember that you didn't want to tell me."

The tips of Ruffino's ears flared red, though the rest of his face was bone white. "I don't appreciate law enforcement trying to intimidate me," he said. "I will be filing a complaint with your superiors."

Grant nodded. "You have that right. But it won't stop me from digging."

Ruffino didn't answer, only glared at Grant until the latter turned and left. He had dealt with the vice president's type before—men used to stonewalling and throwing their weight around—until they ran into someone bigger and harder than they were. They would hide behind their power as long as they could, but in the end Grant would dig out their secrets. He couldn't tell yet if what Ruffino hid was criminal or merely venal, but he thought it might connect to Dane Trask, and that made it Grant's business.

He was halfway down the hall when a familiar figure stepped out of a door to his left. Toby Masterson stopped and watched his approach, his handsome face impassive. "What are you doing here, Commander?" he asked when Grant was even with him.

"My job," Grant said.

Masterson looked past Grant, toward the vice

president's office, the only office at that end of the hallway. "Then that makes two of us."

Grant started to move on, but Masterson's next words stopped him. "Have you seen Eve lately?" Masterson asked.

"You stay away from Ms. Shea," Grant said.

"Or what? You'll have me arrested?" Masterson laughed.

"If you harass Ms. Shea, I will have you arrested," Grant said.

"Oh, I'm pretty sure she doesn't see my attentions as harassment." Masterson leaned against the door-jamb, arms folded across his chest. "But maybe I'll ask her when I take her to dinner tomorrow night."

Fury choked off Grant's words, at the same time his stomach clenched with nausea. Masterson's expression told him the words were no bluff. Eve, who had rejected Grant, had agreed to go out with Masterson, a man she had previously said she was afraid of. The truth of the situation might have buckled his knees if he hadn't braced himself.

He whirled and staggered away down the hall. It felt like a stagger, at least, though his steps were firm and even. Masterson's laughter trailed him all the way out of the building, long after it would have been possible to hear him.

Once safely in his cruiser, he let out a string of curses, forgetting his Lenten vow, forgetting everything but the pain that knifed at his heart.

Chapter Eleven

Several times, Eve had almost called Toby to cancel their date. Only Sarah's encouragement had made her keep the obligation. "You're just jittery because he's so much like Dane," her friend had observed. "It's natural, because Dane really hurt you. But I think Toby is exactly your type. In fact, I think these nerves are your subconscience's way of telling you that."

Under other circumstances, Eve might have rolled her eyes at Sarah's logic, but what did she know? In the past six months she'd been on more dates than she could count where she felt exactly nothing for the man. Feeling something—even doubt—might indeed be a good sign.

Her fear eased a little when Masterson arrived, looked handsome and perfectly respectable in dark gray slacks, a dark gray shirt and polished black shoes. Exactly the kind of outfit Dane had favored. He surprised her by handing her a bouquet of dahlias and lilies. "I figure a woman who owns a florist's shop must love flowers," he said.

She buried her nose in the blossoms, touched by his thoughtfulness. "Don't worry," he added. "I didn't patronize one of your competitors. I stopped by after I was sure you had left for lunch and Sarah helped me pick out something. She said these were your favorites."

"Thank you," Eve said. "Let me put these in water and we can go."

When she returned from the kitchen, Toby was standing by the door, studying a small landscape painting that hung there. She glanced at her desk, a few feet to his right. Was it her imagination, or did the papers there look rearranged?

"You look lovely," he said, pulling her mind out of its paranoia. "Thanks for agreeing to go out with me."

"Thank you for asking."

The modest sedan he led her to surprised her—somehow she had pictured him on a motorcycle, or some expensive muscle car, or even a tricked-out pickup truck like Dane. *He's not Dane*, she reminded herself. That was a good thing.

He took her to a Mexican restaurant with candlelit tables around a central fountain. He was smart and funny and so different from her initial impression of him that she wondered how she could have been so wrong. Over margaritas and chiles rellenos with shrimp, they talked about books and travel, his childhood in California and hers in Oklahoma. By the time the server brought two servings of flan, she was warm and slightly buzzed and thoroughly charmed.

"If I do ever see Dane again, I'm going to have to thank him," he said, looking at her over the candles. "If it wasn't for him, I might never have met you."

She sighed. "I hope he comes home soon," she said. "If only to explain himself. Of all the people I might have guessed would do something like this—wrecking his truck, disappearing—I never, ever would have suspected Dane."

"I'd have said the same thing six months ago," Toby said. "But after you and he broke up, he changed. I think you broke his heart."

Some of the happy buzz faded. "No!" she protested. "It wasn't like that at all." If anything, she had been the one most hurt by the break-up, by the knowledge that Dane hadn't—and never could—love her enough to change his mind about having more children. More than once she had berated herself for holding on to such romantic, even fanciful notions, but she couldn't shake the belief that if Dane had truly loved her, he would have wanted to give her the one thing that would most make her happy. Instead, when she had suggested the split, he hadn't protested at all, merely agreed and started packing the things he kept at her house. That in itself was a kind of rejection.

"Maybe it was just coincidence, then." Toby

scooped up a spoonful of flan. "But about that time he started behaving, well, erratic. Wild mood swings. Paranoia. I even wondered if he was on drugs."

"I can't believe it," she said.

"So he didn't give you any kind of a hint that something else was upsetting him?" Toby asked. "Something at work, maybe?"

"No. Dane liked his job, but he didn't talk about it much. I wouldn't have known what he was talking about anyway. None of that technical stuff interested me."

"So he never talked about the projects he was involved in? I'm surprised. I would have thought he'd want to share that with you."

She shook her head, and took a bite of flan, hoping that would ward off more questions.

"I don't guess he's been in touch with you since he went on the lam," Toby said.

This struck her as such an odd choice of words. She opened her mouth to change the subject but— maybe under the influence of that margarita—she said, "He sent me a letter about a week ago. Well, not really a letter. It was a press release, accusing TDC of falsifying reports or something. It was a wild accusation, with no proof behind it."

Toby sat up straighter. "What did you do with it?"

"I certainly didn't take it to the newspapers. It would have been completely irresponsible." She pushed away the half-finished dessert. "To tell you the truth, the whole thing ticked me off. As if Dane only wanted me to do his dirty work."

"Like I said, he had changed recently."

"I don't want to talk about Dane," she said. This was beginning to feel less like a romantic date and more like an interrogation.

Toby took her hand. "Of course not," he said. "Let's talk about what you would like to do now. We could go for a drink somewhere."

The last thing she needed was another drink. As the effects of the one—large—margarita began to subside, she could feel a headache coming on. "It's late," she said. "I think I'd better go home."

The warmth in his smile didn't waver. "Of course."

At her house, he got out of the car and escorted her up the walk. In the shadows before her front door, he pulled her close, and she didn't resist. She accepted his kiss, and did her best to respond, but even as his lips touched hers, she had a flash of tilting her head up to Grant, feeling his arms pull her close…

She shoved the memory away, and tried to focus on Toby. But the moment felt flat and mechanical. After a few seconds, she eased out of his grasp and he stepped back. "Thank you for a lovely evening," she said, then hurried into the house, disappointment replacing her earlier happiness. Maybe the problem wasn't with the men she dated; maybe the fault lay with her. She had a knack for falling for the wrong men.

THE DAYS WERE growing longer, the evenings less chill, so after work Saturday, Grant decided to go for a run. He hoped a jog along one of the park trails would clear his head and maybe help him come to some insight about this case. And the physical exercise might work off some of the anger and frustration that filled him every time he thought of Eve with Toby Masterson tonight. Logic told him he had no claim on the woman, but logic rarely triumphed over emotion, in his experience.

He changed into running clothes and shoes and set off down the same trail where Marsha Grandberry had been found, her throat cut, Trask's business card clutched in her hand. The crime scene tape and evidence markers had long since been cleared away, and at this time of day in the off-season, Grant had the trail to himself.

But the murder nagged at him like a rock in his shoe. Everything about the scenario felt wrong. Why would Trask kill a random woman he didn't know? There had been no sign of assault or robbery or any concurrent crime. The evidence pointed to a killer who had stepped out of the underbrush, killed the woman and left her for someone to find, with Dane Trask's business card clutched in her right hand.

It simply didn't fit with the picture Grant had of Dane Trask.

So, if he believed Dane Trask wasn't the murderer,

that left the theory that someone else had killed the woman and tried to frame Trask.

But that theory presented plenty of problems, too, not the least of which was, why? The police were already looking for Trask, along with any number of private citizens hoping to cash in on the $25,000 reward offered by TDC. Did the killer think Marsha's death would put even more pressure on Trask? It probably had, but it was a weak motive for murder.

He jogged up the trail, gradually finding a rhythm, feet pounding the soft dirt, breath coming hard but regular and strong, heart pumping. He tried to settle into that zone, mind empty except for his focus on his next breath, his next step.

Something kept distracting him, a feeling that as empty as the landscape appeared, he wasn't alone out here.

He stopped, let his breathing slow, his heart rate return to normal. He took a drink from his water bottle and scanned the scrub oak on either side of the trail. Was that movement in the underbrush in the distance a rabbit or deer, or something more menacing? He knelt and checked the revolver holstered at his ankle, pretending to re-tie his shoe. He liked to think years on the job had given him good instincts, but he felt a little foolish. This place was so empty, but was the killer lurking out there? Was Dane Trask?

And, as impossible as it seemed to him, were Trask and the killer the same person?

He reached the three mile mark on his jog and turned to retrace his steps. Six miles was enough for one afternoon, and he wanted to get home in time to FaceTime with his daughters on the East Coast before too late at night.

By the time he reached the trailhead, orange and pink streaked the sky and the adjacent Black Canyon was already shrouded in darkness. Grant hit the button on his key fob to unlock the cruiser, then slid into the driver's seat. He started the engine and was about to back out when he noticed something stuck under the driver's side windshield wiper. He opened the door and leaned out to snag it, then stared at it, a cold feeling in his gut.

"Welcome Home Warriors," the card proclaimed in red lettering. "Dane Trask" was centered below this, in black letters, along with a phone number.

Grant flipped the card over. In bold black marker on the back of the card was a scrawled message: "I didn't do it."

Chapter Twelve

Grant knew from long experience that cases rarely presented themselves as neatly or smoothly as depicted on television or in the movies. Most solutions came after long, frustrating slogs through piles of data and hundreds of hours of legwork. Many cases were never solved. Accepting this was part of the job, and one he had learned to deal with.

And then a string of seemingly unsolvable cases would come along to strip away all his calm indifference and frustrate him as if he was a rookie fresh from the academy. "We haven't had any luck tracking down the origin of the drawing we found at the dump site," Dance reported at the Wednesday morning meeting to review ongoing work. "We checked the rosters of all the preschools and elementary schools around town, but none of them have a Max registered. We showed the drawing around, but no one recognized it."

"As for the other debris, there's nothing we've

found that ties it to any one location." Beck continued the report. "We think it might even be from several locations."

"Surveillance, both live and with cameras, hasn't turned up anything, either," Dance said.

"Unless you count deer, coyotes and one curious bear," Beck said.

"We think maybe whoever was using the site is done or got spooked and abandoned it," Dance concluded. "We'll continue to check regularly, but right now, we can't justify the resources, and the public lands people are agitating to get the place cleaned up."

"All right, but I want us to have someone there when they start hauling away stuff," Grant said. "Just in case anything turns up."

Beck made a face. "Let's hope it's not a body."

"Unless it's Dane Trask's body," Hud said. "That would solve a lot of problems."

"And create more," Officer Redhorse said.

"Speaking of Trask," Grant said, anxious to move things along. "After I spoke with Mitch Ruffino, TDC handed over some transcripts of calls to their reward hotline that were, essentially, useless." He glanced at his notes. "The usual collection of people who thought they might have seen Trask buying gas or in line at the movies, or hitchhiking out by the lake. None of them could give a solid description of the person they saw, and the descriptions they did give didn't really sound like Trask. One woman said she had seen Trask in a dream, at the bottom of the lake, playing poker with a redheaded woman and a man in a black hoodie."

Laughter traveled around the table. Grant waited for it to subside. "I have a feeling if they got anything less off the wall, TDC is keeping it to themselves. The vice president, Mitch Ruffino, made it clear he didn't want us poking into the company's business."

"I've always felt like they wanted to get to Trask before we did," Beck said.

"Because Trask has dirt on them they don't want us to know?" Knightbridge asked.

"That could be why he left in such a hurry to begin with," Beck said.

"But then why stick around?" Grant asked. "And don't say it's to see justice done, because if that was the case, he would have come straight to us and told us whatever he knew and let us take care of it."

"Commander, there's a call for you on line one." Sylvia's voice interrupted the conversation.

"Take a message and tell them I'll call back."

"Sir, she said to tell you it's your ex-wife and this is an emergency."

The bottom dropped out of his stomach at his words, and he snatched up the phone, aware of the others' eyes on him. "Angela? What's going on?"

"It's Janie. She's run away."

His vision blurred for a moment, and he had to remind himself to breathe. "Run away? When?"

"I found the note this morning. Apparently she left some time in the night. She said she's going to see you!"

A little bit of relief edged out the fear. He had imagined his younger daughter wandering the streets alone, or perhaps with the wrong kind of friends. Instead, she was headed to see him. But there were almost 2,000 miles between her mother's home and his, and a young girl on her own was so vulnerable. "How did she plan to get here? Did she fly?"

"I don't know," Angela snapped. "That's why I called you. You've got connections, haven't you? You can have police looking for her."

"Of course. Have you tried calling her phone? Or texting?"

"She doesn't have her phone with her."

"You mean she left it there? Why would she do that?"

"She doesn't have her phone because we took it away from her, as punishment for breaking her curfew last weekend." Angela sounded as if she was having to force out the words. "That was the punishment we all agreed on—break curfew and you lose your phone."

He wasn't going to argue about the punishment, or spend time finding out why Janie had broken curfew. "I'll start a search for her right away," he said.

"Do you have any idea what she was wearing? What she took with her?"

He made notes of what she told him and promised to get back to her as soon as he knew anything. "Is everything all right?" Dance asked when Grant hung up the phone.

"My fifteen-year-old daughter decided she wanted to come see me and took off in the middle of the night," he said, somehow managing to keep his voice calm. "We need to find her before she gets into trouble."

"If you'll give me the description and photo, I'll put out a bulletin," Dance said.

Grant started to protest that he would take care of that, then thought better of it. The information would probably be better accepted coming from someone who wasn't so closely connected to the situation. "Thank you, Lieutenant," he said. "I'll text everything to you as soon as we're done here."

"I think we've got enough," Dance said. The others nodded.

They left and Dance stood by, waiting. "We'll find her," he said when Grant had given him all the information. "I know that doesn't really help you much." He offered a crooked smile. "My daughter is only nine months old. I can't imagine how I'd feel if she decided to head cross-country on her own."

Grant picked up the phone to call Angela and tell her he'd started the ball rolling, but instead found himself dialing Eve's number. "Hello?" she answered, sounding wary.

"Hi," he said. "I just…" He cleared his throat. "I just heard from my ex-wife that my younger daughter, Janie, decided to take off cross-country to see me. She left a note for my wife and went out sometime last night."

"Oh, Grant!" The words, so full of sympathy and understanding, made his eyes sting.

He swallowed hard. "We're going to find her," he said. "Law enforcement all along her probable route will be looking for her." He couldn't afford to believe they wouldn't spot her. They'd try the airlines, and the bus stations. Maybe the trains, too? He made a mental note to confer with Dance on that.

"Of course you'll find her," Eve said. "And she's your daughter, so she's smart and probably more aware of possible dangers than your average teenage girl. She'll be careful."

Was Janie more aware? It wasn't as if Grant had talked about his work much with the girls. When he had been with them, he tried to shelter them from the ugly side of what he did for a living. Had he talked to them enough about looking out for themselves and being safe? "We'll find her," he repeated. "And then I'll ground her. Maybe until she's eighteen." He forced a chuckle. "It's a good thing I only have two children. Otherwise, I might have even more gray hair."

"Let me know when she shows up," Eve said.

"I will. I just wanted you to know." He started to say more, to ask about her date with Masterson, but stopped himself. That wasn't his business, was it, even though he couldn't stop himself from being concerned about her and her safety. "Thank you for that."

There didn't seem to be anything else to say. He ended the call and stared, unseeing, at the stacks of paperwork in his in-box. He wasn't having any luck finding a man who was hiding out practically under his nose in a national park. How was he going to find a girl who could be anywhere across two thousand miles of country?

EVE HUNG UP the phone, her stomach twisted in a knot. The pain in Grant's voice as he talked about his daughter had reverberated through her. But with it had come the pain of his last words. He was thankful he only had two children.

This isn't about you, she reminded herself. It was about a hurting father, and a daughter who wanted to be with him so badly she was risking a cross-country trip to see him. She said a prayer that Janie would be found safe, and very soon.

Sarah emerged from the back of the store, carrying an arrangement of daisies, delphinium and carnations in each hand. "These are the last two from the cooler," she said, and nestled each vase into a corrugated box designed to keep them from shifting during travel. "Are you sure you want to handle all of these by yourself?" There were six similar arrangements, requiring a series of large delivery boxes.

"If I need help, I'll recruit someone when I get to the school," Eve said. "It's been a long time since I visited and I want to see the new facility that's being built." She also didn't want to lose touch with Audra. Just because things hadn't worked out for Dane and Eve didn't mean Eve wanted to lose his daughter's friendship.

"Well, have fun," Sarah said. "I'll hold down the fort here and finish that batch of corsages." Orders for proms were coming in daily and, knowing the tendency of people, especially teenagers, to procrastinate, Sarah had suggested making up a quantity of corsages in advance that could be finished quickly with ribbon of the buyer's choice, for those who waited until the last minute to shop. It was yet another idea that made Eve pray Sarah wouldn't decide to one day leave and open her own flower shop.

Canyon Critters Preschool sat next door to a busy construction site five miles from the entrance to Black Canyon of the Gunnison National Park. A large sign proclaimed the site as the future home of Canyon Elementary. The small, squat building that housed the preschool was made of sand-colored stucco, which matched the surrounding rock uplifts, so that at first glance the school seemed carved out of the environment. As Eve parked her van near the back entrance, the sound of singing children reached her ears, high-pitched voices chanting the words of a half-forgotten nursery rhyme set to tinkling piano music.

Smiling to herself, she slid open the van's side door and retrieved a rolling cart, onto which she loaded the boxes of flowers. She maneuvered her awkward burden through the back door and down the hallway to an open room. A woman dressed all in red—red tights, red corduroy jumper and a red sweater—looked up from a copy machine. "Can I help you?" she asked.

"I'm looking for Audra," Eve said, and indicated the flowers. "I've brought the arrangements for the luncheon."

"Oh!" She closed the lid on the copier. "I'll get her." She scooted down the hall, a blur of crimson. Eve looked around the workroom, which was crammed with boxes of copy paper, stacks of picture books, foam mats, poster board, the copier, a worktable with a paper cutter and a stapler, and stacks of boxes with handwritten labels for Christmas, Halloween, the Fourth of July, and every other holiday Eve could think of.

"Please don't look, it's a horrible mess." Audra spoke from behind Eve.

Eve turned, smiling, to greet Audra. The woman in red flashed a smile, then squeezed past them to return to her copier. Audra and Eve embraced. "The flowers are beautiful!" Audra exclaimed. "Let me show you where to put them."

When they were well away from the copy room, Eve leaned over and asked. "Why is that woman dressed all in red?"

Audra laughed. "Her class is studying colors. She has an outfit for every color on their list. The children love it." She led the way down the hall to what was clearly a lunchroom, with labeled cubbies, stainless dispensers for milk and juice, and half a dozen large round tables surrounded by plastic chairs in primary colors. A white paper cloth draped the tables, and paper chains hung from the light fixtures overhead, bright and festive. "We'll just put one of these on each table," Audra said, lifting one of the arrangements from its protective cardboard.

"I can do that," Eve said. "I know you're probably busy."

"I'm always busy," Audra said. "But I could use a break. The parents won't arrive for another hour and these things always get me so keyed up, I need something physical to occupy the time."

"Then do you have time to show me your new building?" Eve asked, as she untangled another arrangement from its box. "I saw all the construction when I pulled in."

Audra made a face. "The construction has been a huge pain, but I keep reminding myself that in the end, it will be worth it."

They finished setting out the flowers and Audra stood back and admired the scene. "Everything looks wonderful," she said. "The parents will approve—or at least, most of them will, and that's really the best I can hope for. Some people simply can't be pleased. And the children will love it."

"Let me return this to the car," Eve said, indicating the cart and empty containers.

"I'll go with you and we can walk across to the construction site," Audra said.

The sun beat down, but with the soft warmth of spring, not the intense heat of summer. A light breeze stirred a field of yellow balsam across the street, and cooled the air further. "The day care and preschool are going to be at this end," Audra said, indicating the section of the building huddled up against a massive mound of red and yellow stone. "The back wall will actually be flush with the rock, so no windows there, but the construction superintendent tells me it's going to make for fantastic insulation. He says the design was a finalist for some kind of industry award, so I guess that's good."

They climbed a small hill and skirted around a section of chain-link fencing. "If anyone sees us, they'll yell about us being in here without hard hats," Audra said. "But I don't think they're working today. Actually, I haven't seen anyone over here all week, so I don't know what's up with that, but they're making great progress."

Metal girders and studs, like pieces of an erector set, rose from concrete piers that lined a deep excavation in the rock. Audra walked right up to the edge. "You should have seen all the rock they took out of here," she said. "It was crazy."

Eve stayed back from the edge, not being fond of heights. "The lunchroom and lockers will mostly be in the basement," Audra said. "With some offices and storage. The classrooms will all be up top, with plenty of light. Those rooms without a lot of windows will have skylights, so that everything is sunny and cheerful."

"It looks much larger than your current facility," Eve said.

"Oh, it will more than double our capacity," Audra said. "But they've apparently done studies and they think we'll need it. Lot of young families are moving into the two new developments going up nearby, hence the need for the new elementary school, and the younger children, including children of the teachers, will be able to enroll here. So it will be convenient for everyone."

"And profitable for you," Eve said.

Audra laughed. "That, too. I even accused my dad of pulling strings so that I got the contract for this space, so he wouldn't have to support me, but he denied everything."

"How could your father have influenced that?" Eve asked.

"Because this is one of TDC's projects. You didn't know?"

Eve shook her head. But then, what difference did it make? "I'm sure the fact that you were already here had something to do with the decision," she said. "That, and your school's wonderful reputation."

Audra beamed. "I am really proud of what we've accomplished here." She glanced around and her smile faded. "We'd better go. Somebody is coming and I don't want to get scolded."

She led the way around the fence, but as they started across the parking lot toward the preschool, Eve recognized a familiar figure emerging from the white car on the other side of the construction site. Toby Masterson looked their way and waved, then continued onto the site.

Audra returned the wave. "Do you know him?" Eve asked.

"He's Toby Masterson," she said. "He works for TDC. I'm not sure what his job title is, but he's been over here a lot lately." She shrugged. "He asked me out a couple of times. He's good-looking, but too old for me."

"When was this?"

"The most recent time was last week." She laughed. "I'll say one thing for him, he's persistent. But I'm really not interested in dating anyone right now, you know? Too much drama. I have enough going on in my life. Why?" She nudged Eve. "He is pretty hot. If you're interested in him, I'll put in a good word for you."

"No, that's okay."

Eve tried to push aside the sick feeling in her stomach as she drove back to town. It wasn't as if she and Toby had any sort of binding relationship. They had been on a single date. He was free to see anyone he wanted. Audra was young and beautiful— any man would be attracted to her. But the idea that he had pursued Audra at the same time he was pursuing Eve felt wrong somehow.

She had never had these kind of doubts about Grant. Was it because he was a law enforcement officer? No, she had never believed cops were less vulnerable to corruption than anyone else. But Grant had a way of making her forget her worries when she was with him. Only when they were apart did the worries creep in.

"Did you get to see the new school?" Sarah asked when Eve returned to the shop.

"Oh, yes. It's going to be beautiful. Lots more room." She collapsed and folded the flower carriers and returned them to the storeroom.

When she emerged again, Sarah was looking at her expectantly. "Anything else?" Sarah asked.

"I saw Toby Masterson while I was there." She hadn't meant to say it, but she couldn't keep the information to herself. Sarah would tell her if she was overreacting.

"At the preschool? Does he have children?"

"No, he was at the construction site. TDC is doing the build and I guess he has some role in that."

Sarah leaned across the counter, elbows propped, settling in for a long conversation. "You never said how your date went with him on Saturday," she said. "I've been trying to not be so nosy, but clearly, I'm a failure at that, so how was it?"

"It was okay," Eve said. She forced herself to supply the details her friend would want. "We went to that Mexican place on Main—Mariposa. It was really good."

"So the food was good—what about the companionship?"

"He was nice. Charming and funny. Considerate."

Sarah frowned. "Why do I sense a 'but' at the end of that sentence?"

Eve shrugged. "The evening was nice. But it wasn't special. Maybe I'm just too picky."

"Aww, honey." Sarah's expression softened. "You deserve special. We all do."

"After we saw Toby at the construction site just now, Audra told me he'd asked her out, too," Eve said. "She said he'd really pursued her."

"The way he pursued you." Sarah straightened, watching Eve carefully.

Eve nodded. "The thing is, as nice as the date was, I couldn't shake the feeling that he was trying to get information from me about Dane. Maybe that's why he wanted to go out with Audra, too." Talking about her feelings had helped clarify them, and she realized that this was what had been bothering her all along.

"I think you should trust your instincts," Sarah said.

They both looked up as the door chime sounded and a customer entered. "I'll take care of her," Sarah said. "You take some time to pull yourself together."

Eve nodded, though already she felt stronger, more certain that she was on to something. She went into her office and closed the door, then sat at the desk and dialed Cara's number.

"Hey, Eve!" Cara answered. "Please tell me you've changed your mind about going up to the Mary Lee Mine with me."

"No, but there's something else I needed to talk to you about," Eve said.

"What is it?"

"Do you know a man named Toby Masterson?"

"Yeah, I know Toby," Cara said. "Why are you asking?"

"Did he ever ask you out? Recently? Since Dane disappeared."

"He did! How did you know?"

"Because he asked me out." She didn't mention she'd actually had dinner with him. "And Audra. I think he's trying to find out information about Dane."

"He didn't get anything from me. And he backed

off pretty quick when I pointed out that I'm engaged to an officer with the Ranger Brigade. He probably wants to pick our brains so he can collect that $25,000 reward for finding Dane."

"Did you know Toby at TDC?"

"Only vaguely. I know Dane got him the job there, and that they met through Welcome Home Warriors. But I don't really know anything about him."

Eve sighed. So much for thinking Toby was interested in her for herself.

"You sure I can't persuade you to go with me to the Mary Lee?" Cara asked. "I really don't want to go by myself."

She still didn't want to go, but she believed women ought to stick up for each other. Maybe the three women in Dane's life needed to do that more than most. "All right," she said. "But it's going to be a few days before my schedule is clear. I'll let you know."

"Whenever you're ready. Thanks so much."

Eve waited until the shop closed that evening before she retreated to her office once more and punched in Grant's number. He answered right away. "Have you heard anything from Janie?" Eve asked.

"Not yet." The strain in his voice was heartbreaking.

"Someone will spot her," she said. "We can't give up hope."

"I appreciate the sentiment," he said. "It was good of you to call."

"I wanted to know about Janie, but there's something else, too. Something I need to talk to you about."

"What is it?"

"I don't really want to say over the phone. Can we meet somewhere?"

"Is this about Dane?" he asked.

"It may be connected."

"I'm pretty lousy company right now," he said. "And I don't feel like going out to a restaurant. Can I stop by your house?"

"That would be perfect." She didn't really feel like talking about this in public, either, in case she broke down and embarrassed them both. She hadn't done anything to be ashamed of, but the knowledge that she had, once again, misjudged a man made her feel vulnerable.

Chapter Thirteen

Grant parked in the driveway behind Eve's sedan, again noting the Eve's Garden logo on each side of the car. Red, pink and gold tulips bloomed in the beds in front of the house, lilacs budding behind them. The flowers made the house look like a home, simple and welcoming.

Exhaustion made every step drag, but he forced himself to stand straight and tried to look alert as he rang the doorbell. As much as he wanted to unburden himself to Eve, he was here in a professional capacity. He'd focus on whatever it was she had to tell him that related to his case.

But when the door opened, she took one look at him and held out her arms. He went to her and when her arms tightened around him, the comfort in the gesture left him too moved to speak.

She led him inside, poured a glass of wine and set it and a plate of cheese and crackers in front of him. "I bet you've hardly eaten all day," she said. "And you don't look as if you slept much last night."

"I can't sleep, between worrying about Janie and wondering what got into her head that she decided to do such a foolish thing."

"Fifteen-year-olds behave foolishly," she said. "So do fifty-year-olds, sometimes. So do we all."

He nodded, and sipped the wine, some of the tightness in his stomach easing.

"Tell me what you're doing to find her," she said. "Maybe that will help."

"We've sent Amber alerts, with her picture and description, all over the country, and we've contacted all the airports and bus and train stations, too. We've distributed flyers and I've contacted every law enforcement officer I know personally all over the country and asked for their help."

"Then you have a lot of good people looking for her," she said. "And she didn't just leave to wander the streets. She isn't hiding, not wanting to be found. She's headed here, to see you. So they're going to find her."

He nodded. Everything she said made sense to the part of him that was a law enforcement officer.

The part of him that was father to a headstrong girl wasn't so easily persuaded. "I'm frustrated that I can't do more from this distance. I want to go out and personally look for her."

"You need to be here," she said. "Waiting in case she shows up."

He drank more wine. "Her mother blames me. Her

sister does, too. None of them were happy about me coming here to take this job. But they weren't that happy with me when I lived in DC either." Whatever he had done, it had never been enough for them, he realized. "What is it you wanted to talk about?" he asked.

"I don't think you're going to like what I have to say." She sat hunched, hands on her knees.

"I know you went out with Toby Masterson Saturday night," he said.

She straightened. "How did you know that?"

"I ran into Masterson at TDC on Friday and he made a point to tell me." He helped himself to a slice of cheese and some crackers.

She didn't like that, he could tell. He ate and sipped the wine, watching her. "How was the date?" he asked after a while.

She shrugged. "I should have listened to my initial instincts and turned him down again."

He sat forward, temper rising. "Did he do anything—?"

"No, no. He was a gentleman. But I knew from the first he wasn't right for me."

"Then why did you go out with him?"

She looked away, cheeks slightly flushed. "You're going to think it's really silly."

"Try me."

"After I broke up with Dane, I had this sense of time running out. I'm thirty-six years old. I really want to have a family. A husband and children if possible, but if not, I intend to have children on my own." He didn't miss the lift of her chin, and the note of defiance in her voice.

"There's nothing silly about that," he said.

"That's not the silly part. I told myself that I owed it to myself to do everything I could to find the right man. So I vowed to go out with anyone who asked me. Provided they weren't married or had some other big warning flag against them. I registered with a couple of online sites and I've pretty much stuck with that plan. I've dated a lot of men in the last six months."

"But you haven't found the right one."

"No. And sometimes I get discouraged, but since I couldn't put my finger on any one thing that was wrong with Masterson, I told myself he deserved one chance. After all, what was one date?"

"But now you feel differently." He kept his voice even. Dispassionate. "Why is that?"

"The date was fine at first. I was having a good time, even. But then Toby started asking me about Dane. Why did I think he disappeared? What did the two of us talk about? Did he talk about his work? Had he been in touch with me since he disappeared?"

"He was probing you for information."

"Yes. And then, this morning, I delivered some flowers to the preschool run by Audra Trask, Dane's daughter. She took me next door to show me the site where TDC is building a new elementary school, with attached preschool, which Audra will run. While we were there, Toby Masterson drove up. He didn't speak, but he waved. When I asked Audra if she knew him, she said yes, that he had asked her out several times, as recently as last week. She turned him down but, I don't know, it just didn't sit right with me." She shook her head. "So when I got back to the shop, I called Cara Mead."

"Trask's administrative assistant."

"Yes. And she said Trask had asked *her* out, too. Then I was sure his interest wasn't so much in the three of us, but in what we could tell him about Dane."

"Maybe he's after the reward money."

"He probably is. But it feels like there's something more there than that. After all, he had a relationship with Dane through Welcome Home Warriors. When Toby talks about Dane, I get a sense he feels, I don't know, betrayed or something." She shrugged. "I don't know why I'm telling you this, I just felt you ought to know."

"I appreciate it." He set aside his empty wineglass. "It's good to see you again."

She moved in beside him and took his hand, her skin soft and cool against his own, the soft fragrance of her perfume tickling his senses. "It feels good to be with you, too." She leaned in and kissed him.

Her lips were soft and warm, and she tasted of wine and something faintly sweet, though maybe that was merely his imagination translating his emotions to physical sensation. He slid his arms around her and she pressed against him, the tips of her breasts brushing his chest, vanquishing the weariness that had dragged at him like chains.

She opened her mouth against his and clasped him tighter. He responded by deepening the kiss, trailing his hand down her spine, then stroking the sides of her breasts. He wanted her so fiercely he feared losing control, and wondered if it would better for both of them if he left now.

But he remained fixed in place, kissing and touching, united by longing and joy.

"Come to bed with me," she whispered. "Make love to me. Now."

For a moment he wondered if his imagination had conjured the words. He broke the kiss and looked into her eyes, and found desire as strong as his own reflected back to him. "You're sure?" he asked.

She nodded. "Oh yes."

He wasn't a man who had to be asked twice. He stood, still holding her hand, and let her lead him to her room.

Eve moved with a floating sensation, buoyed by desire—and the heady sensation of taking control. Exactly what felt right. For the past six months—longer even—she had made decisions based on what she wanted for the future.

Tonight, she was doing what she wanted for now.

She wanted to be with Grant. To feel his arms around her, her body entwined with his. To take and give pleasure and savor every sensation without analysis or hesitation.

In the bedroom, she switched on several small lamps, which cast a soft glow in the corners of the room and beside the bed, a simple queen-size mattress and old-fashioned iron frame, topped with a white coverlet. She began to undress slowly. He sat on the edge of the bed and watched. She ignored him, trying not to feel self-conscious, aware of his eyes burning into her.

When she was naked, she walked to the bed and slipped under the covers. Only then did he undress, revealing a body that was every bit as sturdy and muscular as she had anticipated. She felt the power in that body when he crawled into bed beside her and pulled her into his arms, and reveled in the feel of his taut, bare flesh sliding against her own.

Neither spoke, yet she felt an intense communication between them, as he caught and held her gaze, then began to trace the contours of her body with one hand, the other cradling her head. She had the sense that he was memorizing her, learning her the way a blind man might learn unfamiliar terrain.

He shaped his hand to her breast, and when she sucked in her breath as his palm brushed her nipple, he asked, in a hushed voice, "Do you like that?"

"Yes."

He bent and took her in his mouth, and she let out a groan—not of pain, but of pleasure.

Every movement was like that—exploration, discovery, deeper exploration. She followed his lead and began her own expeditions, learning the taste of his skin and the sensitivity of each inch of flesh. Her body hummed with heat and trembled with wanting, impatient for completion yet wanting this sense of being the center of his focus to never end.

By the time he accepted the condom she handed him and unwrapped it, she thought she could hardly bear more pleasure. And then he filled her and she forgot everything that had come before, as he stroked her with one hand, while steadying himself to thrust and withdraw, exquisite friction stoking the fire within until she exploded in light and heat.

He stilled for a moment, as sensation coursed through her in waves. Only when she was still, panting beneath him, did he begin to move again, stronger and deeper, until a second climax like the aftershock of an earthquake shook her, and he cried out with his own release.

Afterwards they slept in each other's arms, the sleep of two people who had no room left to worry about any heartache the future might bring.

Chapter Fourteen

Grant woke to a buzzing noise, persistent and out of place. He didn't want to open his eyes and spoil this pleasant, floating feeling of such peace.

"Grant, your phone." Eve's voice, soft in his ear. She was part of his dream. She nudged his side. "Maybe you'd better answer it."

He opened his eyes, and stared into her face, still soft with sleep, her hair mussed, eyes a little puffy. Yet she was the most beautiful sight to wake up to. He smiled, and she smiled, too. "Your phone," she prompted.

He shoved himself up and turned toward the bedside table, where the phone danced in a circle, like a bumblebee stuck in a flower. The bedside clock showed 7:10 a.m. Too early for a routine call. He snatched up the phone. "Hello?"

"Grant Sanderlin?"

"This is he," Grant said.

"Bryce Larkin, Philadelphia PD."

"What can I do for you, Officer Larkin?"

"I think we may have found your daughter. Or at least, we have a good idea of where she is."

All remnants of sleep vanished. Grant sat up on the side of the bed, heart pounding hard. "Where is she? Is she all right?"

Eve moved in behind him, one hand on his shoulder. The contact made him feel steadier.

"She took the bus from here, headed for Grand Junction, Colorado. Right now she's probably somewhere south of Salina, Kansas."

Relief flooded him, making him weak. He cleared his throat. "Have you spoken to her?"

"No, but we were able to talk to the bus driver and he says she's fine. He's agreed to keep an eye on her until his next stop, which is Denver. I'm calling to see what you want to do then. You could have someone pick her up in Denver, or the bus company people have agreed to keep tabs on her until she reaches Grand Junction. You could pick her up there."

His first impulse was to drive to Denver, to see Janie that much sooner. But his sense of duty told him to stay here, with his active case, and trust others to look after his daughter. "Grand Junction," he said. "If you're sure they'll keep track of her."

"I spoke to one of the head honchos and he promised to put a priority on this. As it was, we were able to track her down because when she bought her ticket, the agent was suspicious and made her fill out her full name and address. She didn't even try to lie."

Grant laughed, as much from relief as anything else. "Thanks for everything."

Larkin gave him the name and number of his contact with the bus company. After Grant talked to the man, he felt much better. He double-checked the arrival time of the bus in Grand Junction and made a note in his phone calendar.

Eve rested her head on his shoulder. "Thank God she's okay," she said.

"How did she get from DC to Philadelphia?" he wondered. "We're going to have a long talk when she gets here."

"When will she be here?" Eve asked.

"I'm going to meet her when the bus gets in a little after five in the morning." He turned and pulled her into his arms. "I want you to meet her while she's here."

Her body tensed. "Do you think that's a good idea? I mean…won't it confuse her, or set up expectations?" She bit her lip, her eyes downcast.

The warmth of the previous night began to seep away. *What about my expectations?* he wanted to say. *Are you telling me I shouldn't have any?* "You're my friend," he said. "That's all she needs to know." He tried for a more cheerful tone. "You can't blame a father for wanting to show off his girl."

She smiled, and if the expression was a little

forced, he chose not to see it. "Of course," she said. "I'll look forward to meeting her."

Relationships—and even relationships that didn't happen—were full of complications. Navigating them was one of the givens of adulthood. And as much as he would have liked to stay in bed and make love to her all day, he stood. "I should probably get dressed and head to the office. I have a lot to do. You probably do, too."

She nodded, and pulled the sheets around her, covering her body as if to say it was off-limits to him now. Why? It was only one of many questions he wanted to ask her, but now was not the time or place for such a discussion. People said all the time that the key to a strong relationship was discussion, but they rarely mentioned how hard it was to make the time for complicated conversations, or how impossible it could feel to find the right words—words that healed rather than hurt, that mended rather than made the rifts worse. Most people weren't cowards, but they all had the instincts to protect themselves from hurt.

AFTER GRANT HAD LEFT, Eve telephoned Cara. "If you're still determined to go out to that mine, I can go with you today," she said. Better to do something active than to sit at home fretting about Grant and his daughter and life in general.

"Yes! I'd love that," Cara said. "And thank you. Thank you so much."

They agreed to meet at Cara's office at one. Eve spent the morning in the flower shop. When Sarah came in at noon, she took one look at Eve and said, "What happened to you?"

"What are you talking about?"

"You just look…different. Happier."

Eve laughed. She was not happy. She was miserable. Grant's phone call first thing this morning about his daughter had brought her crashing back to the reality that he was a man with two children who didn't want more. She felt like the butt of a very mean-spirited joke on the part of the universe. "Nothing has happened to me," she said. "Except we've been really busy. Your idea to make prom corsages ahead of time was genius, but I'm afraid we might even run out of them." She went over the tasks that needed doing that afternoon, then excused herself to meet Cara before Sarah probed further.

Cara greeted Eve with her usual enthusiasm and agreed to drive to the mine, in a truck that turned out to belong to her fiancé, Ranger Officer Jason Beck. "Are you planning to tell Jason about this?" Eve asked as they headed out of town.

"I'm going to tell him tonight," Cara said. "He won't like it, but there's not a lot he can say after the fact. I think he's accepted that, even after we're married, I'm going to do what I think is important. He doesn't seem overly bothered by the idea."

"Times have changed," Eve said. "I remember my father objecting to a trip my mother had planned with friends and she ended up canceling. She said that kind of compromise was part of marriage, but I couldn't help thinking she was the one who always compromised. And my grandfather used to tell my grandmother what to cook for dinner and where she had to shop. And she went right along with it."

"Of course compromise is important," Cara said. "But it's better to work out things together than for one person to be expected to give in."

Eve wanted the chance to build that kind of partnership. As much as she wanted children, marriage was so much more than that. And yes, she wanted it all—love and companionship and a family and a partner for life. Anything less felt like settling. She had tried to explain all that to Dane, but she didn't think he had understood.

"Have you set a wedding date?" she asked.

Cara shook her head. "We know we'd like it to be in the fall, but we haven't pinned down an exact date yet. We want to plan a trip to New Hampshire to meet Jason's parents. And we want to wait until after everything with Dane is resolved. The investigation is demanding so much of Jason's time. I understand that isn't going to change—that's his job.

But with my connection with Dane—we'd just like to have it behind us."

"I understand," Eve said. In a way, her own life felt on hold until Dane resurfaced, or they at least had some explanation for his behavior.

"Hang on, this part gets a little bumpy," Cara said, turning off onto a steep gravel road. They were in the Curecanti Wilderness now, a landscape of yellow and red rock, stunted pinion trees and silvery sagebrush. It looked so barren, and yet as they trundled over the rough road, Eve could make out wildflowers—yellow daisies, red paintbrushes and pink primroses—amid the weeds. Cattle and deer grazed in the distance and a red-tailed hawk wheeled overhead.

They turned off again, onto a narrower gravel road that Eve remembered from when she had attended the protest rally at the mine. That day she had traveled to the mine with six other people crammed into an SUV, everyone chattering and laughing and discussing the plans for the protest. All conversation had ceased when they turned off onto this road, however, since it was so bone-jarringly rough. It was all they could do to hold on and keep from being tossed out of their seats, despite their safety belts.

"Wow, they've really done a lot of work on this road," Cara said as the truck ground up the steep grade. Gravel ticked against the undercarriage as the tires found purchase, but gone were the deep ruts and head-sized rocks they had been forced to navigate before.

"We'll have to park outside the gate, out of sight of the security cameras, and hike in," Cara said. "But don't worry. I know the back way in. We'll get in, collect the samples, and be out in under half an hour."

The nerves that had been hiding beneath their happy conversation now reared up like a monster that had been lying in wait. "Didn't I hear something about you getting shot at one time when you came up here?"

"That was a long time ago," she said. "When I still worked at TDC. The people who shot at me and Jason are behind bars now. They weren't trying to kill us, anyway. They were only trying to scare us off."

Cara talked as if this had happened years ago, instead of only last month. "I'm just a little worried about trespassing," Eve said. "Especially if there are cameras."

"Don't worry. There aren't any cameras where we're going. I checked when we were here for the protest."

They could see the gate now, a massive structure, with tall iron bars extending ten feet on either side of the road. Cara stopped the truck and shifted into Reverse. "The place where we need to park is just back there," she said.

"Wait a minute." Eve craned her head forward to look. "That gate is open."

Cara looked. "Hmm," she said, but continued to back up, turning sharply to take the truck into a gap in the brush, where it would be almost hidden from anyone who didn't know it was there.

They climbed out of the truck, and Cara put on the backpack that contained the sample containers and some other things they might need. She handed Eve a bottle of water and they started into the woods, keeping well away of the open gate and the camera they could clearly see mounted on a post beside it.

After ten minutes of rough hiking, Cara stopped to get her bearings, then turned uphill. "It's just a little way through here," she said.

The ground, though uneven, wasn't too steep, and there was plenty of room to walk between clumps of sagebrush and scrub oak. The air smelled of sage and warmed earth, and if not for the tension that made her jump at every snapped twig or tumbled rock, Eve might have enjoyed herself.

"It's just up here," Cara said, striking out toward a stretch of barbed wire fencing. She looked all around and, apparently satisfied there was no one to see them, stepped on the lower strand of wire and lifted up the top strand. "Go ahead through."

Eve hesitated. "Go on," Cara urged. "We don't want to stand around here too long."

Eve ducked under, then turned to hold the wire for Cara. Her friend led the way along the fence until they came to a cleared area. Cara stopped. "This can't be right," she said.

"What's wrong?" Eve asked, keeping her voice to just above a whisper.

"This doesn't even look like the same place," Cara said.

Before them lay a neat expanse of green interspersed with newly planted saplings, each tree carefully outlined with a little rock wall. Wood chip paths and two iron-and-wood benches added to the feel of a park. "When I was here before—even as recently as the day of the protest—this was all a jumble of rock and tree trunks and old timbers and mining equipment," Cara said. "Not just a few rocks, but a mountain of them. Truckloads and truckloads full."

"Where did it go?" Cara asked.

"They must have hauled it away." She moved forward, down one of the paths. Far ahead they could make out a little stone building. "I remember that building," Cara said. "But nothing else looks the same."

She shook her head. "This whole place is creeping me out. Let's get our samples and leave."

They managed to scrape up enough dirt and gravel to fill two sample bottles, and added water from the creek to a third. Eve wasn't optimistic they would find anything out of the ordinary, but she didn't mention that to Cara, who seemed so upset. "They were supposed to be cleaning up the mine waste, right?" Eve asked.

"Yes, but how could they have done all of this so quickly?" Cara said.

"I'm not sure I understand why you're so upset," Eve said when they were safely back in the truck.

"Dane sent me here because his findings didn't match up with the results TDC was reporting to the government," Cara said. "At least, I'm pretty sure that's why he gave me those two flash drives with reports I think were from here. And when Jason and I came here—the day someone shot at us—the samples we collected then tested positive for a lot of nasty stuff that wasn't supposed to be here."

"Then the protests and your agitating did what they were supposed to do," Eve said. "They forced TDC to literally clean up their act and do what they were paid to do."

"Yes, but…" She shook her head. "It still doesn't seem right."

"Maybe we'll know more after the results of these tests come back," Eve said.

"If there really isn't anything wrong with that site," Cara asked, "why did Dane feel he had to leave?"

Eve said nothing. Only Dane could answer that question, and for whatever reason, he wasn't talking.

"THE DISTRICT ATTORNEY's office has decided to formally charge Dane Trask with the murder of Marsha Grandberry." Faith Martin reported this news to

Grant when he arrived at the Ranger Brigade office Thursday morning after leaving Eve's place.

"On the basis of what evidence?" Grant asked. "We don't have fingerprints or the murder weapon or any evidence tying Trask to Grandberry." They had recovered very little evidence of any kind from the murder scene or the body. No hairs or fibers or DNA, and certainly no witnesses who had seen anyone in the area near the time when Grandberry was killed.

"He was known to be in the vicinity of where her body was found. She was killed with a blade very similar to one he was known to carry. The method of her killing is described in the indictment as one with which he would be familiar." Faith looked miserable as she relayed this news. "I don't think it's a particularly strong case, but public sentiment is very much against Trask, and the DA is under a lot of pressure to indict. Also, I understand TDC Enterprises was one of the chief donors to his campaign, and they've been pressuring for Trask's indictment as well."

Grant had no words to express his disgust over this turn of affairs. "Get me the evidence file for the Grandberry murder," he said.

"Yes, sir." Faith retreated from the office and Grant pulled up the Grandberry file on his computer. There was very little there—an inventory of everything found on the body, including Dane Trask's business card, crime scene photographs, some measurements, the coroner's report.

Faith returned shortly, carrying a cardboard banker's box. "This is everything," she said, sliding the box onto the corner of his desk.

Grant slipped on gloves and began laying out the evidence on the credenza to one side of his desk: Grandberry's clothing, which had shown no sign of sexual assault. Her backpack and its contents: water bottle, map, the wrappings from the sandwich and the core of the apple she had eaten for lunch. The wallet, keys and phone from her pocket. He switched on the phone and keyed in the security code typed on the piece of paper attached to the phone that someone—Hud?—had obtained or figured out.

The home screen showed the usual display of applications and files—messages, emails, photographs, etc. Idly, Grant began scrolling through the photographs. The last pictures she had taken before she died were of scenery—dramatic views into the Black Canyon, vignettes of wildflowers, some artistic shots of the sky.

He stopped at a selfie she had taken in the parking area near the trailhead. A pretty young woman smiled up into the camera, the sign for the trail over her right shoulder. Grant started to move on, then stopped. Over her left shoulder, he could just make out a figure. Was that a person? Another tourist, perhaps? Using his thumb and forefinger, he enlarged the photo as much as possible, but only succeeded in making the background blur. Still, he thought there was something there.

Phone in hand, he went in search of Officer Hudson.

He found Hud at his computer, combing over a printout. He looked up at Grant's approach. "Hello," he said. "I'm just going over the inventory we made of items from that illegal dumpsite. I'm hoping something unusual pops out at me, but so far I'm not having any luck."

"Put that aside for a bit," Grant said. "I need you to work on something else for me." He handed Hud the cell phone. "Take a look at that photograph, will you?"

Hud took the phone and studied the image. "This is the woman who was murdered on the trail, isn't it?" he asked.

"Yes. According to the time and date stamp on that photograph, she took it before she set out on her hike."

"All right," Hud said. "What am I looking for, exactly?"

"There over her left shoulder. Is that another person?"

Hud squinted, then enlarged the image. "I think so," he said.

"Can you enlarge that image and sharpen it up enough to get a clearer picture of that other person?" Grant asked. "Maybe clear enough to get an ID?"

"Maybe," Hud said. "Do you think this might be a potential witness?"

"It might be," Grant said. "Then again, it might be a photograph of her killer."

Chapter Fifteen

The early morning cold cut through Grant's leather jacket as if the garment was made of gauze, but he had forsaken the warmth of the inside of the bus station in order to be that much closer to his daughter's arrival. He shared this chilly space with a man and a woman who both stood at the other end of the building, smoking, and a short woman with a large paunch who had introduced herself as a representative of the bus company, apparently there to make sure he was reunited with his daughter and maybe to persuade him not to sue the company.

More people filed onto the platform as the bus's 5:00 a.m. arrival neared. Grant shifted from foot to foot, not so much to warm his numb feet, but to burn off some of the nervous energy that raced through him. He was exhausted from yet another sleepless night, jittery from too much caffeine and sick to his stomach with worry that something would go wrong and Janie wouldn't be on the bus. Angela had called him at midnight, interrupting the little sleep he had managed to snatch, to alternately sob and berate him for the entire situation. "She gets her stubbornness from you," she said. "She never would have done this if you hadn't encouraged her to be so independent."

Grant had resisted the urge to hang up on her, letting her rant and not saying anything in his defense. He had learned the hard way that responding only riled her more. Better to let her cry it all out, and promise to call her as soon as Janie was safely with him.

The squeal of brakes signaled the big motor coach's arrival. People around him began gathering duffels and tote bags and suitcases. Grant started forward but the bus company rep—Alicia or Felicia or something like that—put a hand on his arm. "Your daughter will get off last, with the driver," she said. "It's already been arranged."

A second employee came out to corral the departing passengers behind a length of yellow tape. With a burst of diesel exhaust and the hiss of brakes, the bus lumbered to a halt. After a few seconds' delay, the doors opened.

The passengers who emerged looked tired and pale, shoulders slumped, feet dragging. They climbed down alone or in twos or threes, men and women, a few children. When at last the bus seemed empty, Grant waited, gaze fixed on the open door. "Where is she?" he asked.

"She's coming," Alicia said.

And then she was there, looking very small and young and a little afraid, her strawberry-blond hair streaming down from beneath a bright pink knit cap. An older man in a bus driver's uniform stood on the step behind her. He said something to her and pointed, and she turned her head and met Grant's gaze.

Her face lit up in a smile that made his heart leap in his chest. And then she was in his arms, hitting him with the force of a wrecking ball, his arms squeezing her tight. "I didn't mean to worry you, Daddy," she said. "I just wanted to come see you, and everything was fine, really."

"We'll talk about it later," Grant said. He tilted her head up and looked into her eyes. "Right now I'm just happy to see you."

"I'm happy to see you, too," she said. "The bus driver told me someone was meeting me here and I was hoping it was you and not the cops." She giggled. "Of course, I guess you are the cops. But I really wanted it to be a surprise."

The bus driver joined them and Janie turned to him. "This is Eddie," she said. "He drove all the way from Dallas and looked out for me."

Grant shook the man's hand. "Thank you."

"You've got a good girl, there," Eddie said. "Never gave me a bit of trouble. Not like some, I can tell you."

Grant thanked the bus company rep and collected Janie's bag. Then father and daughter headed for his cruiser. In the vehicle, Grant handed Janie his phone. "You need to call your mother. She's beside herself with worry."

He waited, not moving, while she telephoned her mother, who greeted her with a wail, then shouting, and finally, tears. "I'm sorry, Mom," Janie said, over and over, tears running down her face. Finally, Grant could stand no more. He took the phone from Janie and said, "It's okay, Angela. She's fine. We're all tired. I'm going to take her home now."

"Her home is here," Angela said, but without much venom.

"She'll call you later," Grant said. "After we've all had some rest." He started the car and headed out, then glanced at his daughter again. "You want to tell me what happened to your phone?"

She squirmed. "I sort of lost it."

"You *lost* it?"

"Mom took it away."

"Because you broke curfew. Why did you do that?"

"It wasn't on purpose!" Her voice rose. "I just sort of, lost track of time. Anyway, it was no big deal."

He struggled to find the right words to say. He hated not being involved in the day-to-day of raising his children—the discipline and tough stuff as well as the good times. But since the girls didn't live with him full time, he had to turn over all of that to Angela. "Your leaving to come here was a big deal," he said.

"I don't know why everyone is so upset," Janie said as they cruised through the dark streets of the still-sleeping town.

"Don't you?" Grant asked. "You aren't smart enough to figure it out?"

He couldn't see her very clearly in the darkness, but he could hear her shifting around. "I wanted to see you, and if I had told you ahead of time, you and Mom wouldn't have let me come," she said. "And it worked out all right. No one gave me any trouble. I always paid attention to where I was, and the people around me, and I always tried to sit right behind the driver, so that if anybody bothered me, the driver could intervene. And I left a note, so everyone would know I didn't run away or do anything stupid."

"Setting off by yourself across the country wasn't very smart, sweetheart," Grant said.

She didn't say anything, but turned her head to look out the window.

"How did you get to Philadelphia?" he asked.

"I took the train. I was going to take the bus all the way, but when I put my starting point and my destination in a trip planner online, it suggested the train to Philly, so that's what I did. It was fun. I'd never been on a train before, or a bus either, except a city bus or a school bus. Traveling across the country is really different."

He stopped at a red light, and studied his daughter in the illumination from a nearby streetlamp. She looked older than she had when he had last seen her, less than two months before, and she had navigated a two-thousand-mile journey with the aplomb of a seasoned traveler. She was growing up, yet she was still a child, her fearlessness a testament to how untouched she still was by the ugliness of the world. He longed to protect her from that ugliness for as long as he could.

She turned and met his gaze and smiled, and he had to look away, so she wouldn't see the sudden tears that stung his eyes. "Where did you get the money for the tickets?" he asked after a while, when they were on the highway, away from town.

"I took it out of my savings account. I know that money is supposed to be for college, but there's a lot in there. I missed you and I really wanted to see you."

Any residual anger melted at those words. "I'm glad you're here now," he said.

She shifted to look out at the passing scenery, bathed in the golden glow of sunrise. "It's so different here," she said. "Very barren and kind of stark. But I like it. Do you like it?"

"I do," he said. "Though it took some getting used to."

"Where do you live?" she asked.

"Not far from where I work, in a little cabin." The cedar-sided A-frame was small, with only two bedrooms and a single bath, but large windows afforded good views of the park and surrounding high plains.

"Do you like your job? Is it very different from what you did in DC.?"

"It's different," he said. "But also a lot the same. I'm still commanding a group of men and women who solve crimes, but here we oversee a bunch of territory and cross a lot of jurisdictions." There was more paperwork and more politics, but also more freedom to do things as he saw fit. The mixture appealed to him.

"So, Dad, do you have a girlfriend?"

The question jolted him. He thought of Eve. He felt closer to her than he had any woman in years, but what were they to each other, really? "You and your sister are the only girls in my life," he said.

Janie rolled her eyes. "Do you have a woman friend? Are you dating anyone?"

"Not exactly." He still wasn't sure where he stood with Eve.

She angled toward him. "Well why not?"

"Why are you so interested?"

"I don't think you should be alone. After all, Beth and I are growing up and we're going to go off to college and probably get married ourselves one day. And Mom remarried. Why shouldn't you?"

Her picture of the future, with her and her sister distant and himself alone, pained him. "I'm busy with work," he said.

"You can't let work get in the way of a personal life," she said, sounding about fifty instead of fifteen.

"I think I can take care of my personal life," he said.

"Well, you haven't been, have you, if you're not dating anyone." She sat back in the seat, a sly smile tugging at the corners of her mouth. "Besides, if you got married again, especially to someone a little younger, I could have a little brother or sister. I think that would be really awesome."

The car swerved, and he forced himself to keep his eyes on the road, Janie's giggles filling the car. He cleared his throat. "Don't you think I'm a bit old to start raising another child?"

"Well, you're old, but you're not ancient or anything. Besides, with modern innovations, you could live to be over a hundred. You've got plenty of time to raise another kid. But you've got to get out there and find a woman to have them."

"You sound like you've got all the answers."

"Just some of them. I read a lot." She said this with such a straight face he didn't dare laugh.

"Tell me about this case you're working on," she said. "The one that's taking up all your time."

"You know I can't tell you about an ongoing investigation," he said.

"Dad!" She sat up straight, her right hand in the air, palm up. "I solemnly swear I won't share anything you tell me on social media or with the press or with any of my friends—who aren't here and don't care anyway. Besides, there's bound to be stuff in the papers already. You can tell me that."

She did have all the answers, he thought. "All right," he said, and told her about Dane Trask disappearing, the accusations against him of embezzlement, and now murder, about TDC Enterprises and the protests at the Mary Lee Mine, and about the frustration of not being able to find a man who was so near yet so elusive.

"Wow." Janie shook her head. "I think I'd have to be pretty terrified to crash my truck and live off stolen food from campers in the desert. Do you think this guy has maybe lost his mind or something like that?"

"I've learned not to make too many assumptions," Grant said. "Anything is possible. We won't know for sure until we find him."

"What if you don't find him?" she asked.

That was one possibility he wasn't willing to consider. "We'll find him," he said. "It's what we do."

"TDC IS HOLDING a press conference at the Mary Lee Mine this afternoon." Eve was in the middle of filling their latest round of prom orders Friday morning when Cara's call came in. "I thought maybe you'd want to go."

"I'm too busy with work to go anywhere," Eve said, passing a spool of purple ribbon to Sarah. "You'll have to tell me all about it."

"We got a fancy invitation in the mail this morning," Cara said. "Wilderness Conservation, I mean.

It says they're going to unveil the newly mitigated mine property. They're rubbing our faces in it."

"You wanted them to clean up the property, right?" Eve asked.

"Sure. But I still can't shake the idea they are up to something shady."

"Let me know how the press conference goes," she said. "Now I really have to go."

She hung up the phone and grabbed another stack of clear plastic clamshells to hold the latest batch of corsages and boutonnieres. But she had boxed up only one when her phone rang again. "What is going on?" she complained, prepared to silence the call until she recognized Grant's number.

"Hello," she said.

She hadn't meant to put any significant emotion into her voice, but Sarah looked over, eyebrows raised in question. *Who is that?* her friend mouthed.

Eve shook her head and turned her back to Sarah. "How are you?" she asked. "How is Janie?" Grant had texted her early this morning to let her know that Janie had arrived safely.

"She's still asleep," he said. "The poor girl is exhausted. I don't think she slept all that much on the bus."

"You're probably exhausted, too," Eve said. "You should try to get a nap."

"No chance of that. I just heard TDC is having a press conference up at the Mary Lee Mine this af-

ternoon. I'll need to be at that. That's why I'm calling, actually. I wondered if you intended to be there."

"No. I mean, we're kind of swamped here at the
shop."

"I thought maybe since you were at the protest
you'd be interested in what they had to say."

"I really only went to the protest as a favor to Cara."

"The thing is, I need to bring Janie with me. I
know that at fifteen she thinks she's all grown up,
but I'm not really comfortable leaving her here by
herself, so far out of town, when my job has such
unpredictable hours. And I thought this might be a
good, low-key way for the two of you to meet."

Of course it would. And she was touched that he
wanted her to meet his daughter. "I'll see if I can find
a way to be there," she said. "I'd love to meet Janie."
And to see you again. But saying that out loud felt
like inviting a jinx. She was enjoying him now. She
didn't want to develop anything with him that de-
pended on the future.

She ended the call and turned back to the flowers, trying to ignore Sarah's stare. Finally, her friend
started, "Are you going to tell me who that was or are
you going to make me beg? And before you answer, I
know that it's none of my business and I'm too nosy
for my own good, but I'm your friend and I really
do care about you. I haven't heard that tone in your
voice or that expression on your face in a long time."

"What expression?" she asked, startled out of silence. "What tone?"

Sarah smiled. "You looked all…dreamy. Soft." She wet her lips. "You're going to kill me for saying this, but you looked in love."

"Oh please! There is no such look."

"There is. And I have to say, I've never seen it on your face before. Not even with Dane."

Eve felt a little sick. Coming from any other person, the words might have been an insult, or a criticism. But Sarah didn't insult or criticize. She only told the truth, even when Eve didn't want to hear it. She tried to focus on the bow she was tying on a corsage, but ended up with the ribbon in a tangled mess. She pushed the flower away. "That was Grant Sanderlin."

"The Ranger commander?"

Eve nodded. "He wants me to come to the TDC press conference at the Mary Lee Mine this afternoon so that I can meet his daughter. She's visiting from DC."

"Awww, that's so sweet." Sarah slid the snarled corsage over and began untangling the ribbon. "You should go. I'll handle things here."

"Sarah, it's too much. You know it is. We're swamped."

"Prom isn't until next Friday night. The kids and their moms won't start picking up the corsages and boutonnieres and hair flowers until that morning. We've got a whole week, and if we work late every night, we can get it all done."

The idea made Eve tired, but she knew Sarah was right. "Maybe I can hire some extra help," she said. "Maybe from a temp service."

"That might be good, but when do you have time to interview someone or post ads or anything?" Sarah asked.

"I'll think of something," she said.

"In the meantime, go to the press conference. Meet Grant's daughter." Sarah's smile turned to a smirk. "So I take it you two have been sneaking around behind my back."

The words—and the expression that accompanied them—surprised a laugh from Eve. "Right. Because you're just too nosy."

"Guilty!" Both women laughed, and Sarah leaned over to hug her. "I'm just happy that you're happy. And I think Grant is a really great guy."

"There's nothing serious going on," Eve said. "We've only been out a couple of times." Though one of those times had been spent entirely at her house, and mostly in her bed. So that didn't exactly qualify as a traditional date.

"You've waited a long time for the right man to come along," Sarah said. "No sense wasting time when he does."

"I don't know about that," Eve said.

"Go to the press conference," Sarah said again. "You might as well meet his daughter and see what happens from there."

Chapter Sixteen

Eve followed a train of cars up the gravel road to the Mary Lee Mine, where men and women in orange safety vests directed them to a level parking area just inside the gate. As when she had been here for the protest, a platform had been set up near the former mine entrance, but instead of a backdrop of piles of rock and broken timbers, now this temporary stage was backed by a row of new saplings and newly sprouted grass.

Eve searched for Grant in the crowd of people who pressed around the stage, but couldn't spot him. She recognized some of her fellow protesters, as well as some TDC employees and people from town.

"Hello, Eve. It's good to see you."

The hair rose on the back of her neck at the words and she whirled around to see Toby Masterson standing behind her. He moved in, uncomfortably close. "I've been trying to call you since our date."

She had silenced every call. After her night with

Grant, she had no wish to see Toby again. Maybe she should have told him that the first time he called, but she'd hoped he would get the message without her having to be so blunt. "I'm not really interested in going out with you again," she said now. "I'm sorry, but it just didn't work out for me."

His expression darkened. "I thought you had a good time."

"I did," she said. "But I'm looking for something...different in a relationship." She cringed at the words. There was really no graceful or truly kind way to do this.

"You're kidding," he said. "I think I deserve at least one more chance."

She shook her head and tried to turn around again, but he took her arm and pulled her to face him once more. "Is there someone else?" he asked. "Someone you prefer instead of me?"

"Let go of me." She tried to tug her arm from his grasp, but he held on tight. "We had one date. I don't owe you anything."

Several people had turned to stare at them now, so he let her go and took a step back. "I'm sorry you feel that way," he said, and left.

She faced forward again, a neutral expression fixed on her face, but her knees shook and she felt out of breath. She had turned down second dates from a lot of men, and been turned down herself. None of those encounters had left her this shaken.

Promptly at one o'clock, TDC vice president Mitch Ruffino mounted the steps and stood behind the podium. "Welcome, everyone," he said. "TDC is pleased to have you witness the unveiling of the results of our hard work at mitigating the Mary Lee Mine. What was once a toxic waste site is now a nature preserve that will be a model for similar projects to come."

He beamed in the roar of applause that followed, though not everyone around Eve was clapping. She noticed Cara standing with Jason, arms crossed, unsmiling.

Ruffino moved to the mic again. "There are a number of people who were instrumental in making this happen that I need to introduce you to." There followed a roll call of men and women in suits and ties who paraded across the stage and waved. Eve went back to scanning the crowd for familiar faces.

Then she spotted Grant moving toward her, a smiling teenager at his side. "Eve, this is my daughter, Janie," he said, stopping before her. "Janie, this is Eve Shea, a friend of mine."

Janie looked from her father to Eve, and her grin widened. She held out her hand. "Pleased to meet you, Ms. Shea," she said.

"It's a pleasure to meet you," Eve said. "How do you like Colorado so far?"

"Well, I haven't seen very much of it," she said. "But what I've seen, I like." She looked around them.

"This looks like something out of a movie. Like a mountain man or a bear could jump out any minute." She slipped her hand into the crook of Grant's arm. "Dad says he's going to take me hiking and stuff when he has some time off."

"Not very exciting for you in the meantime," Eve said.

"No, but it's not like I'd be doing that much back in D.C., either."

"We're trying to decide what she'll do while I'm working," Grant said. "I'm not happy about leaving her by herself while I'm away. But the office really isn't the place for her."

"And I'm way too old for a babysitter." Janie rolled her eyes. "I mean, really!"

"I could use some extra help at the shop," Eve said. "It's prom time and we are seriously slammed." She turned to Grant. "Sarah and I were talking about it just this morning. We need some temporary help, but we're too busy to write out an ad or interview people. Janie would be perfect."

"What kind of shop do you have?" Janie asked before Grant could speak.

"I have a little flower shop in Montrose," Eve said. "The work wouldn't be terribly exciting, but you could help fill orders and answer the phone, and you'd learn a little bit about flower arrangement and plant care. It might be interesting for you. And I'd pay."

Janie's eyes widened. "Dad, that sounds perfect!" she said.

Grant looked skeptical. "Eve, are you sure?"

"I'm absolutely sure," she said, beginning to get excited about the idea herself. "It would solve your problem and mine. I wasn't kidding about needing the help."

"Dad, please!" Janie hung on his arm. "I want to do it."

"All right." He turned back to Eve. "If you're sure."

"I'm sure. You can drop her at the shop at nine, or at my house if you need to get to work earlier. If you need to work after we close, she can come home with me and hang." She turned to Janie. "How does that sound?"

"It sounds awesome." Janie hugged her, a quick, tight embrace that sent a surge of happiness through Eve.

"Thanks," Grant said. "You've taken a real load off my mind."

Cara and Jason joined them and Grant introduced Janie. Jason nodded toward the podium, where another man in a suit had taken over the microphone and was droning on about TDC's great environmental record. "What do you make of all this?" he asked.

"I think TDC is anxious for good publicity after all the negative news over Dane Trask," Grant said.

"They cleaned up this place amazingly fast," Cara said. "Considering the state it was in only two weeks ago."

Jason moved closer and lowered his voice. "It's possible TDC hauled everything from the Mary Lee to that illegal dump site," he said.

"You should test the stuff at the dump site and compare it to the test results we have from here," Cara said. "If they match, that would be proof, wouldn't it?"

Grant nodded. "Do it," he said. "But we may need more than that to build a case."

"Uh-oh," Janie said, looking past her father.

Grant and Eve both turned to look at her. "What's wrong?" Grant asked.

"There's a guy over there who is really giving us the stink-eye." She jerked her head to indicate behind them.

Eve looked over Grant's shoulder and drew in a breath. Toby Masterson was scowling at them, and if looks could kill, they might all be dead right now.

JANIE WAS WAITING on the sidewalk when Eve arrived at the flower shop Saturday morning. She held out a to-go cup. "I hope you like mocha latte. It's my favorite, even though Dad thinks I'm too young to drink coffee." She rolled her eyes. "Even Mom thinks that's silly."

"Thanks," Eve said. "It's my favorite, too."

"See, I knew I liked you." Janie skipped behind Eve into the shop. "Oh, wow, this place is so cool." She sucked in a deep breath, eyes closed, chest expanding. "And it smells so good." She opened her eyes. "I really love flowers."

"I hope you still love them after you've worked with them all day." She led the way to the storeroom and showed Janie where to stash her backpack, then gave her a tour of the shop, naming the various plants and flowers they passed.

"Should I be taking notes?" Janie asked. "I'm never going to remember all of this."

"It's all right," Eve said. "There won't be a test." She switched on the lighted Open sign. "But speaking of tests, why aren't you in school?"

"Oh, my school is on this weird quarterly plan— three quarters on, then one off," she said. "But they're staggered so that some kids go to school while others don't. It's supposed to make better use of resources and keep you from forgetting stuff over long breaks. Anyway, it's my quarter off."

Eve nodded. "All right. I'm going to start you off by going through the loose flowers in the cooler. Pull out any wilted or browning blossoms. Then we'll have room for flowers that come in this morning's delivery." She took the girl to the cooler in the back and showed her how to look for browning leaves and drooping flower heads and set these blooms aside.

"So, what do you think of my dad?" Janie asked. She twirled a daisy, not looking at Eve.

"I think he's a great dad," Eve said. "I know he was really worried about you, and so happy you're here now."

Janie made a face. "I mean, what do you think about him, you know, as a man?" She cast a sideways glance at Eve. "Like, to date."

Eve bit back a smile. Nothing subtle about this kid. "Your dad is a great guy," she said.

"Have the two of you been out? I mean, he introduced you as a friend, but I wasn't sure what he meant by that."

"He meant, I'm a friend."

"He really likes you, I can tell." She dropped the daisy in the bucket they had set aside for flowers to be discarded and faced Eve. "I think you should go out with him," she said. "I know he's older than you, but he's good-looking, don't you think? And I see older guys with younger women all the time. And it's not like you're a teenager or anything. Would it be so weird?"

Eve couldn't help but laugh at this onslaught. "It takes two people to decide to date," she said.

"But I can tell he really likes you. Yesterday afternoon at that press conference thingy, he couldn't keep his eyes off you. But he's probably shy, because of the age difference and you're so beautiful and everything. So I think you should ask him out."

Eve felt her cheeks heat, whether from the information that Grant had been watching her, or Janie's comment that she was beautiful—or the knowledge that she wasn't being entirely truthful with this sweet girl about her and Grant's history. She put a hand on

Janie's shoulder. "Let's just see how things develop naturally," she said. "Okay?"

Janie shrugged, and Eve left her to finish the flowers.

At ten, Sarah arrived, bringing the mail. "Lots of junk, as usual," she said, handing the bundle to Eve. "But there's a letter in there for you." She winked. "It looks personal."

Janie emerged from the back room. "Hello."

"Janie!" Eve motioned the girl forward. "Sarah, this is Janie Sanderlin. She's visiting her dad for a little while and will be helping us out."

"Is your dad the Ranger Brigade commander?" Sarah asked, glancing between the girl and Eve.

"He is," Janie said. "And I'm really excited about working here." She turned to Eve. "Maybe I should have told you before, but the only other job I've ever had is babysitting."

"You'll do fine," Eve said. "Sarah, would you show Janie how to package the prom flowers while I look through this mail?"

"Sure thing," Sarah said. "Come on. We'll get the packaging knocked out pretty quick, and then I'll show you how to make bows."

The pair retreated to the workroom while Eve stood over the trash can in her office, sorting the mail. More than half went straight into the recycling bin, she filed a few bills to pay later and then she finally came to the letter Sarah had mentioned.

The letter was in a thin, prestamped envelope, the kind sold over the counter at the post office. The address was in block printing, but the sight of it sent a shiver up Eve's spine. She picked up a letter opener and slid it under the envelope flap.

Dear Eve,
I haven't seen anything that looked like my press release in the newspapers, so I'm guessing you decided not to pass it on. I was counting on you to help me out, since I'm not really in a position to do these things myself. That's probably hard for you to understand, but I'll explain more after all this is over.

I know we had our problems there at the end, but we had a lot of really good times together before that. I still love you, even if it wouldn't work for us to be together. For the sake of that love, would you help me out here?

No matter what you hear, I haven't done the things they're accusing me of. I can't tell you more because I don't want to put you in any danger. Please believe that.

If you still have that press release, please send it to someone who will dig more into that story. They'll be surprised by what they find.
Love,
Dane

GRANT MADE IT a point to get to the flower shop shortly before six o'clock Saturday evening. As much as he appreciated Eve's offer to take Janie home with her, he wanted to spend as much time as he could with his daughter. Angela had agreed Janie could stay in Colorado until her new semester started in three weeks. He was even trying to persuade Beth to fly out the last week so they could all be together.

Half a dozen people crowded the shop when Grant arrived, and it was several seconds before he spotted Janie in the crush. She stood next to Sarah at a table next to the flower cooler, chatting with people who waited in line and stapling paperwork.

Eve, who stood at the cash register, ringing up sales, looked up as he entered and smiled, but didn't stop working. Grant stepped to one side and waited for the rush to ease.

Ten minutes later, the last customer stepped up to the register. "Dad!" Janie raced across the shop and stopped in front of him. "Is it six o'clock already? I've had the most amazing time."

"Hello, Commander," Sarah said, joining them. "This is quite a daughter you have here." She put a hand on Janie's shoulder. "She's been a huge help to us today. I don't know what we did without her."

"It was fun," Janie said. "Sarah's been teaching me how to make corsages. My bows are still a little lopsided, but I know if I keep practicing I'll get really good at it."

The last customer left and Eve followed them and switched the sign to Closed, then locked the door. She leaned against the door for a moment. "What a day," she said.

"You're not usually this busy, are you?" Grant asked, one arm across Janie's shoulders.

"Prom time. We're getting lots and lots of orders." Eve straightened and came to stand with them. "Sarah had the idea to advertise in the school newspapers and it's really paid off."

"I was telling the commander what a big help Janie has been," Sarah said.

"You did a terrific job today," Eve said to the girl. "I hope you'll come back Monday."

"Of course I will." Janie turned to her father. "That's the plan, isn't it? Please say yes."

He nodded, amused by Janie's enthusiasm for this new job. "That's the plan."

Eve patted Janie's shoulder. "Will you help Sarah straighten up the back room while I talk to your dad for a minute?"

"You bet." Janie raced off, Sarah following in her wake.

Grant turned to Eve. Something in her expression had caught his attention. "Is something wrong?" he asked.

"Come into my office."

He squeezed in, then she shut the door behind him, then picked up an envelope from the desk. "I had another letter from Dane today," she said. "I don't know what to make of it."

Careful to handle the letter only by the edges, he unfolded it onto the desk and leaned over to read it. He cringed inwardly at the declaration of love, but pushed on. "That press release accused TDC of falsifying reports, right?" he asked when he had finished.

"Yes," she said. "But the mine site has been cleaned up. At least, it looks clean. Is he trying to say it isn't?"

"That part about not saying more because he doesn't want to put you in danger," Grant said. "That makes me uncomfortable."

She hugged herself. "The whole situation makes me uncomfortable."

He pulled her close and she rested her head on his shoulder. "Thank you again for taking in Janie and giving her something to do," he said.

"Are you kidding?" She smiled up at him. "She really has been a tremendous help." She laughed.

"What's so funny?" he asked.

"We had a very serious conversation this morning, in which she tried to persuade me to ask you out. She pointed out that, despite our age difference, you are actually pretty good-looking, and going out with you wouldn't be so horrible, would it?"

He wasn't sure whether to be appalled or flattered. "What did you tell her?"

"I told her I thought we'd see how things developed naturally."

He pulled her closer, hands on her hips. "And how would you say things are developing?" he asked. "Naturally?"

Hands on his shoulders, she pressed her forehead to his. "I love being with you," she said. "The other night was…special."

"But?"

She stepped back. "But I want children. I'm not willing to compromise on that."

"I know. And I'm not suggesting you compromise." But he was forty-five. He'd be close to retirement age before any child he had now graduated high school. He'd made so many mistakes with the girls, and they had all suffered for it. How could he go through all that again? "I need to focus on Janie while she's here," he said. "We'll talk more later."

She sighed and looked away. He wanted to pull her close and tell her that everything would be all right. But how could he make that kind of promise when he knew not every problem had a solution, and not every ending was a happy one?

He collected Janie and drove home. Once inside, she dropped her backpack and headed for the kitchen. "What's for dinner?" she asked. "I'm starved."

"How about spaghetti?" He moved to the pantry and took out pasta and a jar of sauce. "There's meat thawing in the refrigerator. Get it for me, okay?" He took off his jacket and shoulder holster and draped them over a chair, then unbuttoned his cuffs and began rolling up his sleeves.

Janie opened the refrigerator and took out the package of ground beef. "You can cook?" she asked.

"Don't act so surprised."

"You never cooked when you lived at home."

"I didn't have to. Your mother is a very good cook."

"Well yeah, but everyone likes a night off now and then, right?"

He winced. Would Angela have liked if he had offered to cook every once in a while? He had never even thought about it. Only when he had been out on his own, forced to learn his way around a kitchen or subsist on takeout, had he really discovered a talent for making at least basic meals. "You can set the table," he said.

He unwrapped the meat and dumped it in a skillet, then set water to boil for the pasta. Janie arranged plates and flatware on the little table in the middle of the kitchen. "I like it here, Dad," she said. "Maybe I should stay."

He could only imagine what Angela would say to that idea. And he was pretty sure the novelty of a new place would give way to the reality of living in a remote area with most of her friends and her mother and sister two thousand miles away. "It's great having you here, Pumpkin, but you need to go home to your mom and sister," he said. "I'm going to miss you, though."

"I can come back after school is out, right?"

"You can come back as often as you like. But no more surprise visits, okay? When you want to come see me, you let me know and I'll buy you a plane ticket."

"It probably would be nicer to fly than all that time on a bus. But it was an adventure, you know? It's good to have adventures."

"You and your sister have certainly been my adventure."

"Ha! That's something, coming from a cop." She looked around. "What do you want me to do now?"

"I forgot to collect the mail on the way in. Check the box, will you?"

She left to check the mailbox, bouncing as she moved, full of energy even after a long day. He watched her go, the familiar tightness of loss in his chest. He was going to miss her when she went back to her mother. The house would be emptier, and so would his life. Raising children was so hard—but he couldn't think of anything more rewarding.

Could he do this again?

He pushed the idea away. Maybe he'd learned some things, but he was still the same person. He had the same job and the same habits, none of which seemed compatible with the demands of raising a family. How often had Angela reminded him of that? He might have fallen out of love with her, but he couldn't deny she was usually right.

Chapter Seventeen

"We got the test results from the dump site." Tuesday morning, Jason Beck dropped a stack of papers onto Grant's desk. "And some new results from the Mary Lee Mine."

"When did you test the Mary Lee Mine?" Grant asked.

Beck flushed. "Someone from Wilderness Conservation took the tests the day before the press conference and forwarded the results to us."

If Grant had to guess, he would pick Beck's fiancée, Cara Mead, as the anonymous tester, but since these results were unlikely to ever end up in court, given their uncertain provenance, he let it pass. "Summarize the findings for me," he said.

"The results from the dump site show some of the same findings as the first tests from the Mary Lee Mine," Beck said. "Traces of uranium and thorium."

"Some," Grant said. "But not all?"

"No, sir. There are a couple of other things—

asbestos, for one—that never showed up at the Mary Lee."

"So we can't be sure the debris actually came from the Mary Lee?"

"No, sir. I believe it did, but we can't be one hundred percent sure."

Grant glanced at the reports. "With these findings, we can't even be fifty percent sure. An expert witness would tear this apart in court."

"Yes, sir."

"What about the latest tests from the Mary Lee?" Grant asked.

"They come back clean. Whatever TDC did up there, they got rid of the bad stuff, in a hurry."

"So they did what they were paid to do. Dane Trask doesn't know what he's talking about."

Beck frowned. "Dane Trask?"

Grant shook his head. "Never mind. Ask Hudson to come see me when he gets a chance."

"Yes, sir."

When Beck was gone, Grant pulled up the copy of Dane's letter that he had scanned in. He had logged the letter into evidence, but he hadn't mentioned it to anyone else yet. He wanted time to try to figure out the significance of the correspondence, if any. Was Trask a nutcase who was fixated on getting his former employer in trouble? Was he paranoid, imagining danger where there was none?

Then again, it appeared the man might have been

framed for murder. That might make anyone wary. As for the embezzlement charges, Grant didn't have enough knowledge of that case to pass judgment, though Dane didn't act like a man who had stolen a bunch of his employer's money. In those cases, the guilty party at least attempted to skip town. Dane kept hanging around, even with a price on his head that had would-be bounty hunters coming out of the woodwork. Apparently, a park ranger had arrested a man just two days ago who was stringing trip-wires across trails in the area of the park where Dane had been most frequently spotted.

Worse than Trask's vague accusations against TDC was his declaration that he still loved Eve. She hadn't commented on that part of the letter. Was that because she didn't care—or because she cared too much?

Two minutes later, Officer Hudson sauntered in. The man walked with a kind of swagger, as if all his joints were a little loose. "Beck said you wanted to see me?" Hud said.

"Any results from that photo from Marsha Grand-berry's phone?" he asked.

"Not yet," Hud said. "But I'm working on it. I've got a computer program that sharpens photos pixel by pixel. It can do some amazing things, but it takes time."

"Let me know as soon as you have something." Ever since he had found that photograph, he couldn't shake the idea that the picture showed something significant. He might be all wrong. What looked like a person might turn out to be a tree, or if it was a person, it might be a tourist from Akron who hadn't seen a thing.

But sometimes in an investigation, you did get lucky. They could use a little luck with this one.

"THANK GOD THAT'S over with for another year." Sarah shut the door to the shop Friday at six and flipped the sign to Closed.

"I can't believe that cooler was full this morning and now it's empty," Janie said, eyeing the cooler that was empty of everything but a few rosebud arrangements and loose flower petals.

"Ladies, we sold one hundred and twenty-five corsages, fifty-seven boutonnieres and two dozen hair arrangements," Eve said. "Definitely a new record."

Janie whooped and Sarah joined in. "Go home, Sarah," Eve said. "Take lots of pictures of Robby and his date."

"I'm on my way." Sarah already had her purse in hand. "I told him he wasn't to leave the house before I got there. And he can't anyway, because I have his keys."

"I can't believe she took his keys," Janie said, as Sarah hurried down the sidewalk away from them.

"I guess parents have to learn how to outsmart their children." Eve sagged back against the counter.

"How do you feel about ordering in pizza for dinner? Your dad texted me that he has to work a little late."

"He texted me, too, and pizza sounds good."

"You don't mind coming to my house with me, do you?" Eve asked. Part of her was looking forward to having the girl over. Over the past week of working together, the two of them had become good friends. Janie was funny and optimistic, and a hard worker, too. Grant deserved part of the credit for that, surely.

"No. I want to see your house," Janie said.

"All right. Do me a favor and stash these roses in the back cooler. I want to shut this one down and first thing Monday we'll give it a good clean-out."

"Sure thing." Janie hugged the four bud vases to her chest and headed for the back room, while Eve leaned into the cooler to flip the switch at the back.

When the door buzzer sounded, she didn't recognize the chime at first, since they were closed and she'd seen Sarah lock the door. Then a hand clamped over her mouth and strong arms yanked her backwards out of the cooler.

"Don't struggle, or you'll just get hurt," Toby Masterson said. The blade of his knife flashed in the overhead lights, then she felt the sting of it against her throat. "You come with me now, and everything is going to be all right."

JANIE EASED OPEN the door of the big walk-in cooler and stood for a moment, searching for a place to put the bud vases. Sarah had explained this morning that flowers like these, that didn't sell by Saturday night, could sometimes be used in other arrangements Monday morning. Rosebuds would be blooming roses in mixed arrangements or for corsages. Longer-lasting flowers like mums and alstroemeria could last a week or more if cared for properly. Running a flower shop was a balance between always offering fresh, beautiful flowers and wasting as little as possible.

She spotted space on a shelf in the back and hurried to put the roses there, then paused to admire the bucket of pink carnations that was all that was left of the stock they had used for prom. Eve had mentioned that next Wednesday she had a huge order of flowers coming in for a big wedding. Janie really hoped she would get to help with those arrangements, and maybe even get to go with Eve when she delivered the flowers to the church and the reception hall. Spending her break here was turning out to be so much more interesting than hanging out at home with Mom and Beth and her friends.

She left the freezer and started back toward the front of the shop when the sound of a man's voice made her freeze. The voice was low—too low to be her dad's. They were closed, so it wouldn't be a customer, would it?

On tiptoe, and holding her breath, she crept to the curtain that separated the workroom from the rest of the shop. She stood right behind the curtain, straining to hear.

She didn't know exactly what she was hearing, but she knew it made her afraid. Scuffling sounds, like a struggle. Then something heavy being dragged over the floor. The man's voice again, the words indistinct, but like he was giving orders. Then the sound of the door opening, the door chime sounding, and then…nothing. So silent she could hear her own breath heaving in and out, and her heart pounding.

After what seemed like forever, but was probably only a few minutes, she eased back the curtain and peered into the front of the shop. The first thing she noticed was the sliding door of the display cooler open. Flower petals littered the floor around it. Had they been there before? Maybe. They had all been pulling things in and out of that cooler all day.

She took two more steps forward, until she could see the whole shop. Empty. "Eve?" she called, almost a whisper. Then, a little louder. "Eve?"

No answer. She wanted to cry, but she forced back the tears. She had to think. What to do? What would her dad do?

Hands trembling, she picked up the phone receiver and dialed. Then she sank to the floor behind the counter, where anyone watching wouldn't see her. "Dad?" she asked when he answered. "Can you come to the flower shop right away? I think something really bad has happened."

THE FURY IN Toby's eyes startled Eve, and the knife in his hands frightened her, but the thought of what he might do if Janie suddenly walked in on him terrified her. So she made no protest when he tied her hands roughly behind her back. He held the knife to her throat again. "You make a sound and I'll cut you," he said. "Do you understand?"

She nodded, and he dragged her toward the door. He gave no indication that he had any idea Janie was in the store, and this knowledge sent a flood of relief through Eve. Janie would probably be confused and frightened when she came back to the front room and Eve was gone, but she had a good head on her shoulders and would probably call her father.

Grant would think of something, she told herself, comforted by the thought. Grant would take care of Janie, and help Eve.

Out on the sidewalk, she stumbled alongside Toby to the white sedan she remembered from their date. Toby opened the passenger door and shoved her inside. "Don't try anything stupid," he said. "I can still hurt you bad."

"I won't," she promised. All she wanted was to get him away from the flower shop before Janie ran out or he spotted her through the front window.

She remained silent as they drove through town and headed toward the national park and the wilderness land that was part of the Ranger Brigade's jurisdiction. "Where are we going?" she asked.

"We're going to find Dane Trask," he said.

"Do you know where he is?" she asked, surprised.

"No. But when he finds out I have you, he'll come running, and then I'll have him."

"I don't think I understand," she said. Why would Dane come running?

Toby grinned. "You don't? Let me put it another way. I'm setting a trap to catch Trask. And you're the bait."

JANIE'S WORDS WERE like an icicle to Grant's heart. "Take a deep breath," he said, as much to his daughter as to himself. "And tell me what's going on."

"I think someone broke into the shop, right after we closed. I was in the back cooler and heard a man's voice, then some thumping sounds and…" She made a sound like a sob. "When I came out, Eve was gone."

"Where are you now?" Grant asked. "Are you somewhere safe?"

"I'm on the floor behind the front counter."

"Do me a favor. Go into the back room. Wait there. I'll be right there."

"I love you, Daddy."

"I love you, too, Pumpkin."

He ended the call, moved into the main room of headquarters, and scanned the men and women working there. "Beck! Dance! With me," he ordered and headed for the armory at the rear of the building.

By the time Dance and Beck reached him, Grant

had opened the locker containing SWAT gear and began passing out body armor, helmets and weapons. "What have we got?" Dance asked, accepting a sniper rifle.

"A possible kidnapping," Grant said. "The flower shop where my daughter is working. She just called to say someone—she thinks a man, but she only heard his voice, she didn't see him—came in after closing. She heard a struggle and when she came out of the back room, the shop's owner, Eve Shea, was gone."

"Eve Shea is Dane Trask's girlfriend," Beck said.

"Was," Grant said. "They split up six months ago."

"Do you think Trask has her?" Dance asked.

"I don't know who has her, but we're going in prepared for anything. After we assess the situation, we may call in reinforcements. Right now, I need to go make sure my daughter is all right."

On the way into town he called the Montrose Police, then dialed the number for the shop. It rang and rang, but finally Janie answered. "Eve's Garden, how can I help you?" She sounded so adult it hurt to hear.

"Janie, it's Dad. How are you doing?"

"I'm okay," she said. "I'm sitting here by the back door with the phone. Nobody else is here."

"We're on our way. The Montrose police are coming, too."

When the two Ranger cruisers pulled onto Main,

two Montrose squad cars were already parked in front of the flower shop. A sergeant met them on the sidewalk. "No sign of activity inside," he said.

"My daughter is in there, in the back," Grant said. "She says no one else is in there. Let me go in first and get her."

"The door's unlocked," a second Montrose officer said. "We tried it, but didn't go in."

Grant pulled on gloves, then went in. Everything looked pretty orderly. The door to the display cooler stood open, and there were a few flower petals on the floor, but otherwise, nothing looked out of place. "Janie!" he called. "You can come out now."

Seconds later, Janie pushed back the curtain that separated the front of the shop from the workroom. She was very pale, and stared at the group of armed men, wide-eyed. "Come here, honey," Grant said, and she ran to him and buried her face in his side.

He hugged her close and patted her back while she cried a little. Dance and Beck and two Montrose officers searched the shop from front to back. "It's clear," Dance said, emerging from the back a few moments later.

Grant gently pushed Janie away and handed her a handkerchief. "Take a minute to calm down, then tell us what happened," he said.

She sniffed and scrubbed at her eyes with the handkerchief, suddenly looking very young. He wanted to pull her close again, to shield her from all the danger and ugliness in life. Instead, he took out a recorder. "I'm going to record this, so we have a record," he said. "You tell me everything you remember."

She started from when she took some vases of rosebuds to the back walk-in cooler, through hearing the man's voice and the sounds of struggle, up to when she called him. Her voice shook a little as she relived it all, but she remained tough. "I couldn't hear what the man was saying, and I didn't recognize the voice, but it was deep—deeper than yours."

He switched off the recorder. "You did a good job," he said. He turned to the others. "Talk to people in the shops on either side and across the street and see if they saw anything."

"We'll start processing the scene for evidence," the Montrose sergeant said.

Janie turned toward the display cooler. "I don't know if those flower petals were on the floor before or not," she said. "But I think Eve was in there when the guy came in and grabbed her."

Grant patted her shoulder. "Try not to worry about it, Pumpkin," he said. "You did what you could— now it's our job to find her." Every second counted. Grant had no idea what Eve's kidnapper intended, but his job was to get to them before the man could act on his intentions.

Chapter Eighteen

"What is going on here? Has there been an accident or something?" A woman's voice rose out on the sidewalk.

"Sarah!" Janie called, and Eve's assistant pushed past one of the Montrose officers and rushed up to them.

"Janie, what is going on?" she asked.

"Eve's been kidnapped," Janie said, and started crying again.

The color left Sarah's face and she turned to Grant. "Eve's gone?"

He took her elbow and walked with her a little way from Janie, who continued to sniffle and mop at her face with the handkerchief. "Janie was in the back room and heard a man's voice and sounds of a struggle. When she came out, Eve was gone and the shop was empty. She said this happened not too long after you left. Did you see anyone near the shop when you left—in a car parked nearby, or on the sidewalk?"

Sarah shook her head. "I didn't notice anyone. But then, I was in a rush to get home and see my son and his date before they left for prom."

"Was there anyone in the shop earlier in the day who acted suspicious? Anyone angry about anything?"

"No. Nothing like that." She glanced at the cops swarming the shop, taking photographs and measurements, dusting for fingerprints. "After my son and his date left, my husband and I decided to go out to eat. We were driving past and I saw all the cop cars and I had to see what was happening."

She turned as a bulky man with a broad face and thinning blond hair came into the shop. "I'm Dale McLean," he said, putting an arm around Sarah. "What's going on?"

"Someone's kidnapped Eve," Sarah said.

Janie joined them and Sarah put her arm around the girl. "You were so smart to call your dad right away," she said.

"I'm worried about Eve," she said.

"I'm sure your father and his men will find her." Sarah looked at Grant. "You're going to be busy a while, aren't you? Working? I can take Janie if you like."

He hadn't even thought about what he would do with Janie while he searched for Eve. He looked at his daughter. "Would you mind going home with Sarah?" he asked.

"I guess not," she said.

"I'm sure you'd rather be at your own place, but I'd appreciate the company," Sarah said.

"All right," Janie said.

She went to the back room to retrieve her backpack. "Thank you," Grant said. "I wouldn't want her to have to stay at my place by herself."

"Of course not. She's a great kid, Commander. You should be proud."

"I am."

After Janie and the McLeans left, Beck and Dance returned, bringing with them a young black woman with close cropped hair and large, wide-set eyes. "This is Isabel Hart," Dance said. "She works at the sandwich shop across the street and may have seen our guy."

Grant fished out his recorder again. "I'm Commander Sanderlin," he said. "Tell me what you saw."

The woman looked around nervously, then said, "I went out to water the flowers in the planters by our door a little after six and I saw a man come in here," she said. "I remember because he shoved the door really hard and made a grunting noise. That's what made me look up. I thought the door must have stuck." She shrugged. "I didn't think a lot about it after that. I went inside."

"Was the sign on the door turned to Open or Closed?" Grant asked.

"I don't know. I think he was blocking the sign so I couldn't see it."

"But you're sure about the time?" Grant asked. "Just after six."

"Yes. Because we have a special that runs from six to eight and I had just rung up my first one of the evening."

"What did the man look like?" Grant asked.

"Tall. Dark hair. Not fat or thin." She shrugged. "His back was to me, so I didn't see his face."

"Thank you, Ms. Hart." Grant switched off the recorder. "We may have more questions for you later. We appreciate your help."

She left and Dance said, "He might have forced the door, or picked the lock. It's a pretty basic lock. There's an alarm, but it wasn't set yet."

"He could have had a key, too," Beck said. "If he'd been in the shop before or knew Ms. Shea, he could have swiped the key or borrowed it and had a duplicate made."

The Montrose sergeant returned. "We've put out an APB with Ms. Shea's description," he said. "We haven't found anyone who remembers any kind of trouble with her and a man, or even a disgruntled customer. No ex-husband in the picture."

"She dated Dane Trask for a couple of years," Dance said.

The sergeant's eyebrows rose. "Maybe he came back for her?"

"The man the woman across the street described fits Trask's description," Dance said.

"We're not ruling out anything at this point," Grant said. He gave the Montrose officer the description Ms. Hart had shared. "Are there any security cameras that might show the area around the shop?"

The sergeant shook his head. "A couple of places have cameras inside, but none of them are focused on the street. We'll keep talking to people, and we'll put out this description, in case anyone recognizes someone."

He left and Grant turned to Dance. "I'm going back to the office. Keep me posted."

On the drive back to the office, he scanned every car he passed, hoping to see Eve, or a man who fit the description Ms. Hart had given. He refused to think what might be happening to her and focused instead on why someone might have taken her. Had Dance returned out of some misdirected version of love, determined to take Eve into exile with him? Maybe the man really had lost his grip on reality.

Eve had no fortune, or wealthy family, so ransom seemed out of the question. Had someone been stalking her, one of her former dates who believed she was in love with him, or even a stranger who had decided he wanted her?

Back at the office, Hud met him just inside the door. "I've got that image you were waiting for," he said. "The one from Marsha Grandberry's camera."

Dully, he followed Hud to his computer and studied the enlarged and enhanced image of a dark-haired man, squinting into the sun. "It looks to me like he's definitely watching Grandberry," Hud said. "Judging by the trees around him, I'd put him at about six-two, approximately 180 pounds." He paused. "He fits the description for Dane Trask."

Some of the fog cleared from Grant's mind as he studied the picture. Though still slightly blurred, the image was recognizable. "It's not Dane Trask," he said. "That's Toby Masterson." The two men did resemble each other, superficially. Looking at this image, it struck Grant that Masterson could have been the man who opened Trask's safety deposit box. He could have used a fake ID, or stolen one from Trask, either at work or at Welcome Home Warriors.

"Who is Toby Masterson?" Hud asked.

"He works for TDC. He knows Dane Trask from Welcome Home Warriors." And he had dated Eve. "It's very possible he killed Marsha Grandberry," he said. "And I think he kidnapped Eve Shea. He fits the description we got from a witness and Eve went out with him at least once, and he's tried to date the other women in Dane Trask's life—Cara Mead and Trask's daughter, Audra. I think he's obsessed with Trask." He clapped Hud on the back. "Get me everything you can on Masterson. I especially want to know the make, model and plate number of the vehicle he's driving."

They were going to get this guy, but how long did they have before it was too late?

MASTERSON SWITCHED OFF his headlights and they barreled down the highway in the darkness. "What are you doing?" Eve cried. Was he trying to kill them both by speeding blindly along these twisted mountain roads?

He didn't answer, but suddenly swerved left, bumping onto a rough gravel road. She tried to make out some landmark in the darkness, but that was impossible. She didn't know how Masterson could even see to drive, it was so dark out, with no moon and few stars and no other light for probably miles. The car rocked wildly from side to side and she tried to brace herself with her feet, but banged her head hard against the side window. "Are you trying to kill us?" she shouted.

He slammed on the brakes, throwing her forward, though the seat belt he had fastened around her kept her from catapulting through the windshield. She strained her eyes to see him in the dark, but could only make out shadows. She thought she heard him breathing hard over the rumble of the car's engine.

He grabbed her, and she cried out, startled, and then in pain, he was squeezing her so hard. "Where is Dane hiding?" he asked. "You must know. You two were lovers. You said he'd been in contact with you since he left. Why? Did he want you to meet him and run away?"

"I don't know where he is," she protested. "He never told me anything. And we're not lovers. Not for a long time."

He shoved her away. "No, you're not Dane's lover. You're sleeping with that cop, that Ranger Brigade commander. You'd do that old man but you could hardly stand to kiss me." He swore at her, then put the car in gear and they rocketed forward once more, but not as fast as before, and after a few seconds, he switched on the headlights.

The high beams illuminated a landscape of rock and sagebrush, the road two faintly discernable ruts climbing steeply. Not the road to the Mary Lee Mine, she thought. "Where are we going?" she asked.

"I know a back way into the park," he said. "We're going to look for Dane." He sounded calmer now. More sane.

She assumed he meant the National Park. "It's a big park," she said. "How will you find him?"

"Because I've got you. He'll want to save you. He's got a hero complex, did you know that? It's why he started Welcome Home Warriors. He wanted everyone—all the townspeople, and all of us veterans—to look up to him. That Dane Trask, what a great guy." He laughed. "People aren't saying he's so great now."

"But Dane did help a lot of people," she said. "He helped you get a job with TDC."

"I got that job on my own," he said. "Dane just took credit for it."

Was that true? She tried to remember, but she hadn't paid that much attention.

"And then he stole all that money from TDC," Toby continued. "Everybody thought he was such a hard worker, winning all those awards, and putting in all those long hours, when in fact, he was siphoning off money from the jobs he worked."

She started to protest that that didn't sound like Dane, but could TDC really make those accusations without proof? Toby continued talking. "When he found out everyone was on to him and he was going to be arrested, he tried to fake his own death, pushing that truck into the canyon. But then he was stupid enough to keep showing up. He couldn't lay low and keep quiet. People like him, always wanting to be in the spotlight, can't ever do that."

The Dane she had known and loved hadn't been one to seek the spotlight. He had never been shy or timid, but he never went out of the way to tout his own achievements. Had love blinded her to his faults?

"The people at TDC were on to him for a long time," Toby said. "But they had to be careful. They had to collect a lot of proof. I talked to one of the people who was investigating Dane and he told me all kinds of things they found out about him. They said he was selling drugs to some of the guys at Welcome Home Warriors. Some of those men and women were fighting addiction and instead of helping them, Dane was making money off their weakness. Disgusting."

Eve listened, dazed, trying to take it in.

"The guy at TDC told me they thought Dane had a secret safety deposit box where he kept records of all this stuff. I did some snooping and figured out where it was, but when I looked inside, it was just a bunch of pictures and stuff. He was too cagey to keep anything incriminating, I guess."

"You broke into Dane's safety deposit box?" She shifted to face him, even though she could see him only dimly in the light from the instrument panel. "How did you get the key?"

His teeth flashed white as he grinned. "Dane mentioned once that he had given you a key. I don't remember how it came up, but I went to your house while you were at work one day to look around. You really should have better security. A woman living by herself can't be too careful."

She felt sick, knowing he had been in her house, had pawed through her things. And to think she had kissed this man!

"And then he murdered that woman. Everybody said they didn't see it coming, but I did. I knew he had that kind of violence in him. You didn't believe me when I tried to warn you, but now you see it's true, don't you?"

She didn't answer. She couldn't.

"Don't you see?" Toby's shout reverberated through the darkness. "He has to be stopped. The police won't do it. Your precious Ranger commander won't do it. So I have to do it." He wrenched the car off the road, careening wildly.

"Stop!" Eve screamed. "You'll kill us both!"

He braked hard, skidding and slamming into a rock outcropping. The airbags exploded, filling the air with choking white dust. Eve felt the impact against her chest, and bowed her head, eyes watering, disoriented in the darkness. In the sudden silence her own ragged breathing filled her ears. The driver's door opened with a metallic protest, and a cold breeze raised goose bumps on her arm. Then her own door opened and Toby pressed his knife to her chest.

She went rigid, steeling herself for the first cut. But instead of stabbing her, he sawed at her seat belt, then dragged her from the car. "Come on," he said. "We walk from here."

Chapter Nineteen

"Masterson's car isn't at the airport or the bus station or the train station." Lieutenant Dance stood at the front of the room, briefing the members of the Ranger Brigade, as well as Montrose County Sheriff's deputies, Colorado Department of Public Safety officers and Montrose Police Department officers who had mobilized to search for Toby and Eve. Men and women filled every seat in the Sheriff's Department classroom, and stood shoulder to shoulder along the walls, many clutching cardboard cups of coffee. Grant had positioned himself in a back corner, arms crossed over his chest, jaw clenched. "We checked hotels in Montrose, Delta, Grand Junction and all the surrounding communities and the car isn't there," Dance continued. "We've alerted gas stations, campgrounds and any other place they might have gone. We're drawing a blank."

"He could have taken her to a private residence," a woman in the crowd said. "If the car is in a garage somewhere, we'll never see it."

"Masterson rents an apartment midtown," Dance said. "We've had the place staked out since shortly after he took Ms. Shea. He hasn't been there. He hasn't been in contact with friends, family, or people he knows from work. We put a trace on his cell phone, but the battery is either dead or he's removed it. In any case, he hasn't used it to make any calls, and he hasn't purchased anything with his credit cards."

"What's his history?" a man asked. "Has he done anything like this before?"

"He's got a couple of domestic violence charges dating back three years," Dance said. "Both involving physical altercations with a woman he was dating at the time. They were both charged. But nothing since then."

"Somebody said he dated Ms. Shea?" someone else asked.

"He went out with her one time that we're aware of." Dance looked to Grant for confirmation. Grant gave a curt nod. "Her coworker at the flower shop said she recently turned him down for a second date," Dance continued.

"Maybe he didn't like that," a woman said.

"Maybe not," Dance said. "Right now, we don't care about his motivation so much unless it gives us a clue as to where he is now."

"We need to focus on the National Park," Grant said.

The rustle and creak of uniforms and weaponry

filled the room as everyone shifted to look at him. Grant pushed his way toward the podium. "Grant Sanderlin, Ranger Brigade Commander," he introduced himself. "Masterson was obsessed with Dane Trask. He tried to date Trask's administrative assistant and his daughter, and only succeeded with Ms. Shea, who had a long-term relationship with Trask that ended six months ago. New evidence has come to light this evening that leads us to believe it was actually Masterson who murdered Marsha Grandberry in the park, and left one of Trask's Welcome Home Warriors business cards on the body in an attempt to frame Trask. Masterson and Trask worked together at Welcome Home Warriors, so Masterson had easy access to those cards."

"What evidence?" a man asked.

"Ms. Grandberry took a selfie with her phone at the trailhead, just before she set out on her hike. An enlargement of the photograph shows Masterson standing nearby, watching her."

A murmur spread around the room. "It's a big park," someone in the back said. "Where do we start?"

Grant pulled a map of the park from his jacket and pinned it to the wall behind him. He used a pointer to indicate a section ringed in yellow highlighter. "We've had several confirmed sightings of Trask in this general area. We think Masterson may take Ms. Shea here, in an effort to lure Trask out of hiding." It was, at best, an educated guess, but for now it was all they had.

He stepped back from the podium, and Dance took over to assign areas for the various groups to patrol. Grant left the room, signaling to Carmen Redhorse to accompany him. "I'm headed to the Dead Horse Trail," he said. "Masterson killed Ms. Grandberry there, so he may return with Eve. I want you and Knightbridge as backup."

"Yes, sir," Redhorse said. "Are we going in on foot?"

"Yes." It was a risky move, carrying with it the danger of being ambushed, but in that rough country, he didn't see any other approach to take.

"If I may, sir, I think we should send officers in from both sides in a flanking maneuver," she said. "It's rough country there, but it is possible to approach from the south and east."

"Good idea. No more than a couple in each group," he said. "We don't want to sound like a herd of buffalo closing in on him."

"No, sir."

He left her to the details and returned to his cruiser. He sat, the engine and lights off, the radio turned down so that the chatter was a low murmur. He had called Janie and talked to her before going into the sheriff's department, and she had sounded tired, but calm, and had seemed okay with spending the night with Sarah and her husband, but had made him promise to call her as soon as he found Eve. Her faith that he would find Eve, and that she would be all right, buoyed him.

He closed his eyes and tried to put himself in Masterson's shoes. He couldn't think what the man was thinking, only try to predict based on past behavior. Masterson projected an air of swagger and confidence, which sometimes was a blind for deep insecurities. He and Trask had worked together, had maybe even been friends. Trask had helped Masterson find his job at TDC. Unlike others of Trask's friends, who had defended him when he was accused of theft and murder, Masterson had on more than one occasion tried to persuade people—particularly Eve—that Trask was dangerous.

Possibly, Masterson was jealous of Trask, of the respect and admiration Trask had received. He wanted that respect and admiration for himself. He wanted the life Trask had led.

He wanted the woman Trask had loved.

Grant wondered what an FBI profiler would think of his theories. He didn't have time to wait for a profiler's opinion. He could only act on his own instincts, and his instincts told him Masterson would bring Eve to the national park—to taunt Trask or maybe to trap him. But Grant intended to get to him before he had a chance to do either.

EVE DIDN'T KNOW how long they had been stumbling along in the dark, over boulders and through brambles, falling and getting up and falling again. After her fifth fall she had persuaded Toby to untie her hands. "There's nowhere I can run to out here," she said. "And I can balance myself a lot better if I can use my hands. I'll be able to move faster."

"All right, but if you try to run away, I'll kill you," he said, with all the emotion of someone explaining to a five-year-old that failing to clean his room would result in a lost allowance. He flashed his knife again to cut her free, and she winced as she brought her arms forward and rubbed feeling into them.

"Come on," he said, and grabbed her arm and dragged her after him again.

After what seemed like an hour of walking, the ground became less rocky, and stunted junipers and oaks replaced the sagebrush and weeds. Eve wondered if they were near the rim of the Black Canyon, then wished she hadn't thought of that. In the darkness it would be so easy to stumble into that black void, and fall for many minutes before hitting bottom.

At that moment, Toby shoved her to the ground, then crouched beside her. "What is it?" she asked. But then she heard it—the steady throb of a helicopter, flying low.

"Keep your head down," he said. "Don't look up. We don't want them to see us."

She pressed her forehead to the ground and closed

her eyes. Was the helicopter looking for them? How would it ever find them down here in the darkness?

The throb of the chopper grew louder and louder, then receded, never passing directly over them. When they could no longer hear it, Toby stood and pulled her to her feet. "Come on," he said. "Let's go."

A short while later she sensed another change in the terrain. Though it was darker than ever, the little moonlight that was available blocked by trees crowding in around them, the ground was smoother underneath. "Are we on a trail?" she asked Masterson, who hadn't spoken in perhaps an hour.

"You get an A," he said. "Clever girl."

A trail meant they were in the developed area of the park. Development meant people. Hikers wouldn't be out this time of night, but would park rangers?

Janie would have alerted Grant to her disappearance by now. Eve couldn't know how much the girl would have heard or seen from the back room, but Grant would be looking for her. How would he ever find her here in the park, miles from the flower shop and even miles, by now, from Toby's car?

She looked up, trying to gauge from the sky how many hours they were from dawn. More people would come to the park with light—climbers and hikers, campers and anglers. With them would come a better chance of being spotted. She just had to hang on until light.

Toby stopped so suddenly she plowed into his back. He grabbed hold and held her against him, an embrace she didn't welcome but could do nothing to fend off. Not without risking the knife he still carried in one hand. She could feel it now, resting against her left shoulder. "What was that?" he whispered, his breath hot in her left ear.

"What?" she asked.

"Listen!"

She listened, holding her breath, and heard…nothing. "I don't hear anything," she said after a long moment.

"I heard something," he said. "Over to our left." He gestured to the side of the trail.

Was it Grant? she wondered. Had he somehow guessed where she was?

"Maybe it's Dane," Toby said.

"That's what you wanted, isn't it?" she whispered.

"Not yet," he said. "This isn't the right place for it." He released his hold on her and shoved her forward once more. "Come on. We have to keep going."

"WE'VE GOT SOMETHING from the aerial mapping the Forest Service chopper crew did." Hud approached Grant at the Dead Horse trailhead, where he and his team were assembling.

"What is it?" Grant grabbed the report and pulled his reading glasses from his shirt pocket.

Hud leaned over his shoulder. "That little red blob

there—that's a heat source. It could be a couple of deer or an elk bedded down, but where it's located, the chopper crew thinks it was people—possibly one big one, but maybe two. They weren't moving."

"They probably heard the helicopter and froze," Grant said. He tried to hide his disappointment. It might be Eve and Toby, but the information was too vague to tell.

"There's more." Hud flipped to a second page in the report. This was a fuzzy black-and-white photograph of what looked like a wrecked car. "They got this, about a mile and a half from the heat source," Hud said.

Grant squinted at the photo. "It's hard to tell much about it. Maybe it's been there a long time."

"Uh-uh," Hud said. "They spotted it because they were getting a heat reading from the engine. It was still warm. And it gets better." He turned to a third page. This was a close up, blurry but legible, of a license tag. "That's the tag number for Masterson's car. For whatever reason he abandoned it and started walking. They're headed this way."

Grant let out a breath, feeling twenty pounds lighter. "All right, everyone," he said in a normal tone of voice. "Let's get in place. We've got confirmation that our targets are headed this way."

"What's the plan?" Dance asked.

"I want you positioned across the trail, about 100

yards out, hidden in the brush. I need two officers on this side of the trail."

"Spencer and Reynolds are on their way," Dance said. "They should be here soon."

"Radio them to position themselves near the trail, about fifty yards apart. I'm going to be on the trail. If I can intercept Masterson, you three can close in from both sides. Redhorse will be behind me, about fifty yards farther south on the trail. Hud will be fifty yards north. Remember, he's got a hostage, so do everything you can to avoid endangering her. I'm gambling we can catch him off guard."

Plans made, they moved toward their positions to wait and pray they could stop Masterson, before he killed again.

Hold on, Eve, Grant sent a silent message. *I promised Janie I'd bring you home safe.* He had never made a promise he wanted to keep more.

Eve was tired, her body heavy, every step an effort. They must have walked miles over rough country, and that after working on her feet all day, then being terrified for most of the night. "I have to stop and rest," she told Toby. "I can't keep going."

"You can sleep when you're dead," he said, with no hint that he was making a bad joke. "Keep going."

"But where are we going?" She didn't move. She didn't think she could. She sank to the ground. "I need water, and food," she said. "I haven't eaten since breakfast." The shop had been too busy to stop for lunch, though she had insisted Janie eat the sandwich Grant had sent with her.

Masterson knelt beside her and pulled a water bottle from his pack. She unscrewed the lid and drank, the water so good and cool going down. He took a long drink, too, then dug a protein bar from his pack and passed it to her. He took one for himself as well and for several minutes they ate in silence.

"Do you think that helicopter earlier was searching for us?" he asked.

"Probably." She saw no sense in lying. Masterson wasn't stupid. "But they couldn't have seen us. It was too dark."

"They use infrared," he said. "We did some of that in the army, looking for insurgents. They use it to map forest fires and stuff, too. It operates on heat signals. You can spot a person in pitch black from 800 feet in the air with those things."

The last bite of the protein bar stuck in her throat. Did that mean the helicopter had seen them? That it knew where they were? She tried to hold onto the hope that bloomed within her, but it died too quickly. Rescuers might know where she was, but Toby still had that knife, and he was close enough to kill her with one thrust.

"Did you take the picture I had in my office of me and Dane?" she asked. "The one of the two of us in a field of lavender?"

He didn't speak for so long she started to repeat the question. "You looked so beautiful in that photograph," he said. "So happy. When I saw it, I realized how completely Dane had fooled you. I took it so you wouldn't be reminded of him."

As if she could forget a man she had been with for three years simply because his picture was gone. But Toby's sudden honesty made her bold. "Did you kill Marsha Grandberry?" she asked.

"What?"

She forced the words out. "Did you kill Marsha Grandberry? That college girl whose throat was cut on the trail?"

"No! Dane killed her. He left his business card so everyone would know he did it. That's how messed up he is."

Masterson worked with Dane at Welcome Home Warriors. He would have had access to Dane's business cards. And he wanted everyone to know how terrible Dane was. "I just wondered," she said. She forced herself to stand despite her wobbly legs, suddenly anxious to move. If they kept going on this trail, they would eventually reach a trailhead, and a road. And someone who could help her.

Toby rose beside her. "You believe me, don't you?" he asked. "Dane killed that girl, not me."

"Of course," she said. But he was the one with the knife. He had held it to her throat and she had believed he had been ready to kill her.

They moved again, Masterson just behind her, almost stepping on her heels with each stride. She walked with her head down, trying to see where she was going, an impossible task in the darkness, though overhead, above the trees, the sky had lightened from charcoal to ash.

She sensed more than felt movement somewhere to her left, and lifted her head to listen. Had it been a deer, or a large bird—or a person? She glanced back at Toby, but he gave no indication he had heard. So she kept walking, ears straining for any hint of sound. Twice more she thought she might have heard something, but when no one appeared and Toby didn't react, she told herself she was imagining things.

Then a dark shape loomed, ten yards in front of them. "Police! Freeze, with your hands up!"

She tried to comply, lifting her hands in the air, but Masterson tackled her from behind and dragged her back against him. She felt the sting of the knife at her throat. "Don't move or she's dead," he shouted.

"You're surrounded, Masterson." She recognized Grant's voice now. "You'll never get away alive. Don't make things worse on yourself."

"If Eve dies, her blood is on your hands, Commander!" he shouted. The knife pricked, and a hot dampness bloomed. She closed her eyes, willing herself to stay strong, to push back the panic.

"We know you killed Marsha Grandberry," Grant

said. "We have a picture of you with her at the trail-head."

"No one would believe how dangerous Dane Trask is," he said. "I had to show you how dangerous he is." His hand shifted, and she gasped as the knife nicked her again.

"Eve, are you okay?" Grant asked.

"She won't be okay much longer if you don't let us through." Toby's voice sounded ragged, higher-pitched. "Get back."

The shadow receded a little. "I'm moving back," Grant said. "Don't do anything rash. We can talk."

"I want you all to back off," he said. "I want you to let me go."

"You have to let Eve go first," Grant said.

Toby laughed, a wild, choking sound that sent a chill through Eve. "That's not going to happen," he said. "Do you think I'm stupid?"

The explosion deafened her, and the back of her head was wet. She fell forward, Toby collapsing with her. She struggled away, to her knees. Then Grant was lifting her, cradling her. "Eve, are you all right?" he asked.

Was she all right? She put a hand to the back of her head and felt something sticky, but there was no pain. "I don't know," she said.

"I need a medic here!" Grant shouted, and two men rushed forward, pulling her from his arms and shining lights on her. Others rushed past her to Toby, who lay crumpled on the ground behind her.

One of the medics shone a light in her eyes, while the other probed at the back of her head. "Hang on a minute," the second man said. "This is gonna be wet, and probably cold." He dumped what must have been a half gallon of water over her, drenching her hair and the back of her shirt, then handed her a dry T-shirt. "You're gonna want to take a shower when you get home," he said. "But none of that blood and other stuff was yours. You're gonna be just fine."

Grant moved forward to hold her close once more. "You're sure she's not hurt?" he asked the medics.

"She's okay. Just blowback from the other guy."

She tried to turn to look at Toby, but Grant held her head. "You don't want to see," he said.

"What happened?" she asked.

"He was shot in the head," he said. She could feel him shaking. "It wasn't a shot I'd have risked in a million years. It was way too close to you. But the shooter knew what he was doing, I'll give him that."

"He must have had a hell of an infrared sight." A man in a visored helmet and body armor joined them. He raised the visor and she recognized Lieutenant Dance. "It wasn't one of our guys, Commander."

Grant shifted her in his arms and faced Dance. "Are you sure about that?"

"I'm positive. Reynolds and Spencer were covering that side of the trail and they got held up by a deep gully they had to navigate in the dark. They didn't show up until after Masterson was shot."

"Someone was trailing us, to my left, for a long way down the trail," Eve said. She cleared her throat.

"It wasn't one of us," Dance said.

Both men looked at her. She closed her eyes and opened them again. "Dane had a sharpshooter's medal from the army. And he had a bunch of guns. He took me with him to the shooting range a couple of times, but I didn't really like it."

"You think Trask shot Masterson?" Grant asked.

"I don't know," she said. "But I think he would have risked a shot like that. To save someone he cared about."

"I'm going to see what I can find out," Dance said, moving past them.

Grant kept his arm around her, and together they walked back down the trail. Eve leaned on him heavily, exhausted, wet and cold, trying not to think about what might be clinging to the back of her.

Grant took her, not to her house, but to his. He showed her his shower and she stood under the hot water until it ran cold, the spray forceful and stinging, washing away some of the horror of the evening, and a lot of her tears. When she finished, she found he had laid out a stack of thick towels, and a T-shirt and sweatpants that were several sizes too big for her, but soft and warm and smelling of fabric softener, and of him. She held the shirt to her nose and inhaled deeply, wanting to stay in this warm, humid sanctuary forever.

But a growing chill and her growling stomach forced her to open the door and step into the hall. She found her way to the kitchen, where Grant stood over the stove, scrambling eggs. "You can make the toast if you want," he said, nodding toward the loaf of bread laid out beside the toaster. "I called Janie and let her know you're okay. She was really worried."

"Poor kid." She fed two slices of bread into the toaster. "How is she doing? I was terrified she was going to come out of the back room while McMasters was there."

"She's a little shaken up, but she's a real trouper. She called for help right away and gave us the information we needed to find you."

"She probably saved my life, and I'll be sure she knows it."

"Sit down and we'll eat." He had made tea, too, and she drank a large mug of it, sweetened with honey, and ate scrambled eggs and toast with strawberry jam and neither of them said anything until their plates were clean. Grant carried the dishes to the sink, then sat across from her. "Do you want to talk about it?" he asked. "You'll need to make a statement at some point, but that can wait if you're not ready."

"It's all right. I can talk about it." Talking was better than silently reliving the events of the night in her mind, though she imagined she would do her share of that, too. She told him everything from the moment Toby had grabbed her in the flower shop.

"He actually told you he wanted to use you as bait to get to Trask?" Grant interrupted when she got to that point in her story.

She nodded. "Yes. I don't know if he envied Dane or resented him. He had read or been told all this terrible stuff Dane had supposedly done, and I think he really believed it. Maybe he felt betrayed by that. He thought Dane needed to be stopped and he was the person to do it."

"I guess it worked, to a point," Grant said. "He managed to lure Dane out of hiding."

"We don't know that," she said.

"No, but we know someone killed Toby Masterson. Someone who was expert enough to risk that kind of shot. You don't take that kind of risk for just anyone."

She bowed her head. If what he said was true, Dane had saved her life. She didn't know how that idea sat with her. Not that she wasn't grateful to be alive, but it was a heavy debt.

Grant slid his hand over hers. She turned her palm up to twine her fingers with him. "I know you still love Dane," he said.

She jerked her head up, startled by the words. "No! What makes you think that?"

"The two of you were together so long. After

you broke up, you admitted you couldn't find anyone else, even though you dated a lot of men. I read that last letter he wrote you, where he said he loved you…"

"Maybe he loves me, but I don't love him. Not in that way." She leaned toward him, compelling him to look into his eyes. "I love you," she said. "Not Dane."

He squeezed her hand tighter. "I love you, too," he said.

Her smile felt as wobbly as her voice sounded. "Then I guess we're both really screwed," she said.

"What do you mean?"

She let go of his hand and leaned back. "I only seem to fall in love with men who don't want children."

He cleared his throat. "About that—I'm man enough to admit I was wrong."

She couldn't speak, only stared at him, waiting. He took her hand again. "I love you," he said again. "And I want to have children with you—if that's what you want."

"You said you had raised two children and couldn't handle any more."

"I lied. Having Janie here with me proved that. I thought I wasn't cut out to be a father, because I'd done such a poor job with Janie and her sister. But she's a great kid, and she loves me in spite of everything, so I must have done something right. I'd like to have a chance to do even better this time around."

"You're not just saying that to get me back in your bed?" she asked.

He laughed, and she laughed, too, breaking the tension. "I love you," he said a third time, and kissed her. "And I think you'll make a wonderful mother."

She buried her face in his shoulder and they held each other for a long time. "It's a little scary," she said after a while. "Marriage and children and the whole nine yards."

"Yeah," he said. "It's a gamble, but I'm feeling lucky. Aren't you?"

She looked into his eyes, shining with love, and couldn't stop smiling. Right now she felt like the luckiest woman in the world, not only because she had survived, but because she had found what she had been looking for, for too long. She thought—she hoped—that it had all been worth the wait.

* * * * *

Look for more books in
The Ranger Brigade: Rocky Mountain Manhunt
miniseries by Cindi Myers,
coming soon from Harlequin Intrigue!

COMING NEXT MONTH FROM

HARLEQUIN
INTRIGUE

Available December 29, 2020

YOU CAN FIND MORE INFORMATION ON UPCOMING HARLEQUIN TITLES,
FREE EXCERPTS AND MORE AT HARLEQUIN.COM.

HICNM1220

SPECIAL EXCERPT FROM

(H) HARLEQUIN

INTRIGUE

*When Raleigh Wilde reappears in
Deputy Beckett Foster's life asking for his help clearing
her name, he's shocked—even more so when he learns
she's pregnant with his child. But a killer is willing
to do anything to keep Raleigh from discovering who
embezzled millions from the charity she runs…*

Read on for a sneak preview of
The Fugitive *by Nichole Severn.*

Raleigh Wilde.

Hell, it'd been a while since Deputy United States Marshal Beckett Foster had set sights on her, and every cell in his body responded in awareness. Four months, one week and four days to be exact. Those soul searching light green eyes, her soft brown hair and sharp cheekbones. But all that beauty didn't take away from the sawed-off shotgun currently pointed at his chest. His hand hovered just above his firearm as the Mother Come First foundation's former chief financial officer—now fugitive—widened her stance.

"Don't you know breaking into someone's home is illegal, Marshal? That voice. A man could get lost in a voice like that. Sweet and rough all in the same package. Raleigh smoothed her fingers over the gun in her hand. It hadn't taken her but a few seconds after she'd come through the door to realize he'd been waiting for her at the other end of the wide room.

It hadn't taken him but a couple hours to figure out where she'd been hiding for the past four months once her file crossed his desk. What she didn't know was how long he'd been waiting, and that he'd already relieved that gun of its rounds as well as any other weapons he'd found during his search of her aunt's cabin.

"Come on now. You and I both know you haven't forgotten my name that easily." He studied her from head to toe, memorizing the fit of her ersize plaid flannel shirt, the slight loss of color in her face and the dark rcles under her eyes. Yeah, living on the run did that to a person. Beckett buttoned his holster. He wouldn't pull. Of all the criminals the United ates Marshals Service had assigned him to recover over the years, she as the only one he'd hesitated chasing down. Then again, if he hadn't cepted the assignment, another marshal would have. And there was no y Beckett would let anyone else bring her in.

Beckett ran his free hand along the exposed brick of the fireplace. otta be honest, didn't think you'd ever come back here. Lot of memories d up in this place."

"What do you want, Beckett?" The creases around her eyes deepened as e shifted her weight between both feet. She crouched slightly, searching ough the single window facing East Lake, then refocused on him.

Looking for a way out? Or to see if he'd come with backup? Dried ss, changing leaves, mountains and an empty dock were all that were there. The cabin she'd been raised in as a kid sat on the west side of lake, away from tourists, away from the main road. Even if he gave her ead start, she wouldn't get far. There was nowhere for her to run. Not n him.

"You know that, too." He took a single step forward, the aged wood r protesting under his weight as he closed in on her. "You skipped out your trial, and I'm here to bring you in."

"What was I supposed to do?" Countering his approach, she moved kward toward the front door she'd dead-bolted right after coming inside kept the gun aimed at him. Her boot hit the go bag she stored near the hen counter beside the door. "I didn't steal that money. Someone at the ity did and faked the evidence so I'd take the fall."

"That's the best you got? A frame job?" Fifty and a half million dollars. e. The only one with continuous access to the funds stood right in front m. Not to mention the brand-new offshore bank account, the thousands ire transfers to that account in increments small enough they wouldn't ter for the feds and Raleigh's signatures on every single one of them. had a choice, Raleigh. You just chose wrong."

Don't miss
The Fugitive *by Nichole Severn,*
available January 2021 wherever
Harlequin Intrigue books and ebooks are sold.

Harlequin.com

HIEXP1220